Buch 683-3946
1537 West Loveland Ohio 45146

THE CLUE OF THE BLACK KEYS

Terry Scott, a young archaeology professor, seeks Nancy's help in unearthing a secret of antiquity which can only be unlocked by three black keys. While on an archaeological expedition in Mexico, Terry and Dr. Joshua Pitt came across a clue to the buried treasure. The clue was a cipher carved on a stone tablet. Before the professors had time to translate the cipher, the tablet disappeared—and with it Dr. Pitt! Terry tells Nancy of his suspicions of the Tinos, a Mexican couple posing as scientists, who vanished the same night as Dr. Pitt.

The young detective is plunged into an adventure that demands all her ingenuity and bravery as she and her friends follow a tangled trail of clues that lead to the Florida Keys and finally to Mexico. Again, Carolyn Keene has woven a suspense-filled story that will thrill her millions of readers.

Was the fluttering handkerchief a signal of distress?

NANCY DREW MYSTERY STORIES

The Clue
of the
Black Keys

BY CAROLYN KEENE

PUBLISHERS   *Grosset & Dunlap*   NEW YORK

Contents

*The Clue
of the
Black Keys*

CHAPTER I

An Urgent Request

NANCY Drew's eyes sparkled as she and Bess Marvin stepped from the afternoon plane.

"Wasn't it a grand weekend in New York?" Nancy said. "But it's good to be back in River Heights. There's your mother, Bess."

Mrs. Marvin kissed the girls and offered Nancy a ride home.

"Thank you," she answered, "but I left my car here."

As the slender, titian-haired girl walked toward the lot with her small suitcase, a young man in a gray topcoat signaled her to wait. His worried look and the urgency of his pace gave Nancy the feeling something was wrong.

"You are Nancy Drew?" he asked. When she nodded, he said, "Your father—"

"Is Dad—is something the matter?" Nancy interrupted fearfully.

"I'm sorry. I didn't mean to frighten you. Your father is all right. But I'm concerned about a friend," the stranger went on. "I consulted your father about him this morning. Mr. Drew said my case sounded more like a mystery for a detective than for a lawyer!"

Nancy studied the eager young man. He was not more than twenty-five, tall and attractive, with serious, blue eyes and reddish hair.

"Perhaps I should introduce myself," he said. "My name is Scott—Terence Scott, but my friends call me Terry. I'm on the faculty of Keystone University. You may think it's strange, my coming to meet you here. But when I learned how clever you are at solving mysteries—"

"I'll do what I can," Nancy promised.

Though still in her teens, Nancy had earned a reputation as a clever sleuth.

"It's quite comfortable in the waiting room," she said. "Suppose we go in there and you tell me your story."

As soon as she had locked her suitcase in her car, they found a secluded bench in the main building beyond a group of waiting passengers. Terry Scott removed his topcoat, folded it, and placed it on the bench between them.

"The story," he said, "begins in Mexico. I was with a group of professors working there last summer to unravel an ancient mystery. Our search led us to an unexplored area, where we planned to dig for a treasure."

"Yes?" Nancy said, her interest aroused.

"According to old legends, something of great benefit to mankind is secreted with the treasure. We professors—Dr. Graham, Dr. Pitt, Dr. Anderson, and myself—are as interested in finding out what this is as we are in finding the treasure."

"You have no idea what it is?" Nancy asked.

"No. After weeks of excavating, Dr. Pitt and I came across a clue which the four of us were sure would lead to the treasure."

Terry Scott leaned forward, his face tense. "It was a stone tablet. We knew at once that all we needed to do was translate the cipher on it, and the secret would be ours. But then something terrible happened."

"What?"

"The night the day of our find, Dr. Pitt and the stone tablet disappeared!"

"He stole it?" Nancy asked, shocked.

Terry Scott frowned. "I don't know. Dr. Pitt was pretty secretive. He is a bachelor, and close-mouthed about his work. But he's a fine teacher, and all the professors would swear he's honest."

"Perhaps he was the victim of foul play," Nancy suggested. "Did you call in the police?"

"Yes. They haven't turned up a thing, but I feel that Dr. Pitt is alive."

"Being held captive somewhere?"

Terry Scott shrugged. "Whatever it is, I mean to get to the bottom of it. Dr. Pitt must be found. And I don't intend that anyone else shall get the credit for something that belongs to us professors!" The young man's eyes blazed.

"I can't blame you," Nancy agreed. "Have you any clues to help solve this mystery?"

"Yes. After Dr. Pitt disappeared, I found a couple of things in his tent that I believe are important. Here is one of them."

He reached deep into a pocket of his topcoat and brought out an object wrapped in tissue paper. It was the bottom half of a large, ancient key, black in color and of an unusual luster.

"There were three of these keys originally," he explained, "all made of obsidian."

"That's glass, isn't it?" Nancy asked.

"Yes, a kind of volcanic glass," Terry Scott answered. "The other keys disappeared when Dr. Pitt did."

He held the curious half-key up to the light for Nancy's examination, then returned it to the pocket of his topcoat.

"We'll need the other half of the key before we're through," he stated. "But, in the meantime, I figure what we ought to do is find a man named Juarez Tino."

"Why?" Nancy asked.

Terry Scott said that he suspected the man and his wife of being the thieves. They had been working near the Mexican campsite for some time before the stone tablet had been found.

"The Tinos passed themselves off as scientists, but my guess is they're fakers. The same night that Dr. Pitt, the cipher stone, and the keys disappeared, the Tinos vanished."

"You think Dr. Pitt went off with them?" Nancy remarked.

"Either with them or after them. I believe if we can trace Juarez Tino and his wife, we'll find Dr. Pitt as well as solve our ancient mystery."

"Oh, I hope so," said Nancy. "Did any of you make a copy of the cipher on the stone tablet?"

The young man shook his head ruefully. "We found the tablet at the end of the day when we were tired. We never thought it might be stolen before morning!"

Suddenly Terry Scott glanced at his wrist watch. "I almost forgot!" he exclaimed. "I promised Dr. Graham I'd phone him. The old man gets very upset if he's kept waiting. Excuse me for a moment, please."

Leaving his coat at Nancy's side, Terry Scott dashed off to a telephone booth around the corner. Nancy waited, pondering the events he had related.

A dark, swarthy man sauntered over and took Scott's place on the bench. Out of the corner of her eye, Nancy saw the man fingering the professor's topcoat.

"What are you doing?" she cried, jumping up and snatching the coat from him.

The man stood up hastily and hurried toward a side door. Just as he disappeared, Terry Scott returned. He noticed Nancy's look of apprehension.

"Is something wrong?" he asked anxiously.

"I'm not sure," Nancy answered. "A man who came to sit here acted as if he wanted to steal your coat."

A frown came over the young professor's face. "What did the man look like?"

"Dark, short," she replied. "Sort of a crooked mouth and beady eyes."

"That sounds like Juarez Tino, the man I was telling you about!" Terry Scott snatched up his coat and plunged a hand into the inner pocket. "It's gone!" he gasped. "Juarez has the black key!"

"We'll go after him!" Nancy rushed for the door through which the man had gone.

Terry dashed after her, and they hailed a policeman Nancy recognized as Sergeant Malloy of the River Heights police force.

"Sergeant," she asked excitedly, "did you see a short, dark man come out of the waiting room?"

"You mean the one that was running, Miss Drew? He just drove off in a blue sedan with another fellow." Malloy waved toward a departing car.

"He's a thief! We must stop him!"

"What are you doing?" Nancy cried out

The policeman and Terry Scott followed Nancy as she raced for her car. The two men piled in beside her, and they sped off.

Nancy drove northward along the main highway toward River Heights, and at last came close enough to note that the sedan ahead had a Florida license plate. Then, at a busy intersection, she was stopped by a traffic light and lost sight of the other car.

"Keep pushing," Malloy directed her when the light changed. "They're up ahead some place."

A few minutes later Terry Scott pointed excitedly. "They just passed us—going the other way! They're heading back to the airport!"

Nancy maneuvered her car in a neat U-turn and took up the chase again. The sedan was well ahead, but Nancy kept gaining. Another quarter mile and they would overtake Juarez Tino.

But just as she approached the far side of the airfield, the blue sedan suddenly swerved from the road. Swaying dizzily, it swung across a rough field and onto the runway. Nancy started to follow, then jammed on her brakes. Her car screeched to a stop, but the sedan kept on directly in the path of an incoming plane.

"There'll be a crash!" Nancy cried out.

CHAPTER II

A Suspect Escapes

NANCY covered her face with her hands, expecting to hear the ripping, grinding sound of a collision. Instead, she heard Terry Scott shout:

"They made it!"

Looking up, Nancy saw the plane taxiing along the runway.

"That crazy driver just missed by the skin of his teeth!" Malloy exclaimed.

"Somebody's getting out of the car," Nancy remarked.

"I'll get him," the sergeant said, opening the door.

"I'll go with you," Nancy offered.

"You two stay here," the officer ordered. "It's too dangerous on the runway."

Nancy bit her lip in vexation. From her first mystery, *The Secret of the Old Clock*, through her most recent, *The Secret of the Wooden Lady*,

Nancy had shown that she possessed courage and daring beyond her years. But she always paid heed to the wisdom of her father and others of his generation. Now she obeyed Sergeant Malloy's order and waited in the car.

The officer reached the sedan on the runway. A second man stepped out of the car.

"Must be the driver," Terry Scott commented. "He's too tall for Juarez."

The policeman leaned inside. Apparently Juarez was not there.

"Juarez must have escaped!" Nancy gasped.

"With my key, the rat!" Terry fumed.

Nancy frowned and turned to her companion. "Are you sure Juarez was in the sedan when it passed us on the road?"

"Yes. Both men were on the front seat."

"Then Juarez must be here at the airport," Nancy declared.

With one hand shielding her eyes from the glare of the sun, she studied the tall grass that fringed the far side of the runway.

"Look!" she cried. "He's running toward the airport building!"

Nancy backed her car onto the road, and headed for the building. Traffic was heavy, and she chafed at the delay, but finally she made it.

As Nancy parked, she and Terry heard the roar of an outgoing plane. A crowd of onlookers were waving good-by.

"Must be that Florida Special I saw chalked up on the flight board," Terry remarked.

Florida! An idea flashed into Nancy's mind. The plane was bound for Florida—and the license on the blue sedan was Florida! Was there a connection?

"Let's go to the ticket office and inquire about the passengers," she said excitedly. "Juarez Tino might be on that plane!"

Nancy quickly gained the attention of a clerk. "May I see the list of passengers who boarded the Florida plane?" she asked.

"Certainly."

She was handed a typewritten sheet. Six passengers had boarded the plane at River Heights. Juarez Tino was not one of them.

"Did all the passengers with reservations claim their seats?" Nancy asked.

The girl at the counter chuckled. "Yes, all the passengers got on. But one of them almost didn't make it. He came rushing up at the last minute, out of breath."

Nancy leaned forward excitedly. "What was his name? Please tell me. I have a particular reason for wanting to know."

The clerk tried hard to remember. Then she pointed to a name on the list. "Conway King. His wife kept fidgeting, worrying where her husband was and commenting in a loud, brassy voice."

"Did you see her husband when he came in?"

The clerk shook her head. "He went right out to the plane. Somebody said he made it all right. That's all I know."

"Thank you," Nancy said, and turned away. When she and Terry Scott were alone, she said quietly, "Do you think Juarez might be using the name Conway King?"

"It's quite possible. And that 'brassy voice' certainly sounds like his wife. I think we should inform the police so Juarez can be questioned at the next stop."

Nancy looked at the flight schedule which had not yet been erased from the board. "The plane won't come down for two hours. Before we tell the police, I think we should make a thorough search for the key."

Her companion looked puzzled.

"When you didn't find the key in your pocket, we both assumed Juarez had stolen it," Nancy reminded him. "But maybe—"

She did not finish the sentence. Beckoning him to follow her, Nancy walked over to the bench which they had occupied earlier. It was possible, Nancy thought, that Juarez had dropped the key in his haste to leave. He might even have hidden it, intending to come back later.

Hurriedly Nancy looked along the top of the bench. No key there. And it was not on the floor underneath. Finally she turned to Terry Scott, who was also searching.

"Are you sure you didn't take that key into the phone booth with you?"

"I'm quite certain. But I'll look just the same."

While he was gone, Nancy examined the floor from the bench to the side door through which Juarez had made his exit. She looked on the ground outside the door. No key.

Disappointed, she returned to the bench and sat down. Suddenly Nancy realized that the dark wooden seat was not solid, but built of strips about half an inch apart.

With renewed hope she felt along the cracks of the smooth wood. Her little finger discovered something. Looking closely, Nancy saw an irregular black object wedged between the boards!

Terry Scott's antique half-key!

Taking a nail file from her purse, Nancy dug out the relic and presented it to the young man upon his return. He could hardly believe his good fortune.

"You're a cool detective! I'm sure that from now on our case will prosper."

Nancy was amused by the word "our," but merely said, "I'm afraid I haven't been very helpful so far. I was only two feet from the man you want to catch, and let him get away!"

"But you proved something," Terry Scott insisted. "I know now that Juarez is on my trail. He probably has learned about the half-key and means to steal it. Also, you discovered that he's on his way to Florida with his wife, and that they travel under an assumed name."

"We don't know that for certain," Nancy reminded him. "We're only guessing."

The young professor laughed. "Now I'm sure you're a lawyer's daughter. That careful, logical mind! Well, how about it? Will you stay on the case and help me solve my puzzle?"

Nancy's curiosity was thoroughly aroused. But nice as Terry Scott seemed, she must check on him first. Nancy decided to talk the matter over with her father.

"If you'll tell me where you're staying, I promise to let you know soon," she replied.

Reluctantly the young man accepted her decision, saying he was staying at the Claymore Hotel. Then, after thanking her, he went to call a taxi.

As Nancy walked across the parking lot toward her car, she heard a shout. Sergeant Malloy was sternly leading an angry, gesticulating man. Nancy recognized him as Juarez's companion—the man who had driven the blue sedan.

"Arrest me, will you?" he roared. "It's this girl—you said her name's Nancy Drew—she's the one you ought to arrest!"

CHAPTER III

Clue in a Triangle

NANCY looked at the heavy-set man in amazement. Sergeant Malloy protested, "Come, now. What do you have against Miss Drew?"

"Plenty," he answered, his gray-green eyes flashing. "She sent you to embarrass me. Look how everybody's staring at me, as if I was going to jail. She's hurt my good name. I've been doing business in River Heights and people know me. My reputation is worth money. My business—"

"What kind of business?" interrupted the sergeant.

"I sell citrus fruit for the Tropical Sun Fruit Company of Florida."

Sergeant Malloy grumbled, "Let's see your driver's license and car registration."

The man thrust them under Malloy's nose. Nancy and the sergeant studied them together. The license and registration were made out to

Wilfred Porterly on a street in Miami, Florida.

"All right, Mr. Porterly," said the sergeant. "Tell me one thing. Where's your friend?"

"Juarez Tino," Nancy added.

Porterly blinked and hesitated, then said, "I don't know any Juarez Tino."

"How about the man who rode in your car? Is his name Conway King?" Nancy asked.

The man's eyes narrowed. "I never saw him before. He begged a ride. Told me he'd left some important papers at his hotel. Couldn't find a taxi, so he asked me to take him back to town.

"After he picked up his papers, I drove him here to the airport. He made me drive onto the field so he wouldn't miss his plane."

"And you nearly killed yourself and all the plane passengers just to accommodate a stranger?" Malloy said sarcastically.

"It wasn't my fault. He grabbed the wheel."

Nancy pretended surprise. "You say Juarez took the wheel?"

"Sure. I mean—I don't know what his name was."

Porterly must have felt that his words had trapped him. He turned his fury on Nancy.

"You're responsible. If there'd been a crash, you'd have been to blame!"

"Nancy Drew," stated a firm, angry voice from the crowd, "is a very fine girl. You'd better be careful what you say about her."

Nancy turned in astonishment. An athletic-looking, dark-haired girl was striding toward her. She was Nancy's friend, George Fayne. With her was pretty Bess Marvin, her cousin.

"What is it all about?" Bess whispered when they reached Nancy's side. "I found I'd left my hatbox, so I asked George to drive back here with me."

"Tell you later," Nancy said in a low voice.

"You'd better quiet down," the sergeant was telling Porterly, "or I'll arrest you for disturbing the peace. Sell all the grapefruit you want, but behave yourself. I'll be watching you."

Porterly hesitated. Then, with a baleful look, he turned and walked rapidly toward his sedan.

Sergeant Malloy spoke to the crowd. "All right, folks, break it up." With a wave of his hand at Nancy and her friends, he strode off.

George Fayne watched the disappearing figure of the blustering Porterly.

"Hypers, Nancy," she scolded, "you do get mixed up with the strangest characters."

"Nancy, you aren't involved in another mystery before you even get home!" Bess exclaimed.

"Well," Nancy confessed, "I'm not sure."

The three girls walked together to Nancy's car and she stepped in.

"We have company," George whispered.

Nancy looked through the rear window of her car. Terry Scott was hurrying toward her and waving an arm. Nancy introduced him to Bess and George.

"I'm sorry about that rumpus with Porterly," Terry began. "I was in a booth trying to call a taxi. I heard shouts, but I hadn't any idea you were involved."

"No harm done," said Nancy. "My friends here came to my defense."

"And we mean to keep on defending you until we get you safely home," George promised.

Terry grinned. "Since your friends protect you so well, perhaps you'll drive me to my hotel. Every public taxi in this town seems to be busy."

"I guess it'll be safe." Nancy laughed.

As the car rolled toward River Heights, Bess and George drove directly in back of her. When she pulled up in front of the Claymore Hotel, Terry reached into his pocket and brought out the tissue-wrapped half-key.

"I want you to keep this for me," he said to Nancy, "both as a pledge of my integrity and because I no longer dare keep it myself."

"You mean someone like Juarez may try to steal the key?" Nancy asked.

Terry nodded and said, "This must never get in the hands of the wrong people. Please take my case," he went on. "I believe that you are the person who can solve it."

Nancy hesitated to take the key until she knew him better, but decided to show it to her father when she asked his advice about the case. Aloud she said, "You'll hear from me tomorrow."

Nancy slipped the relic into her shoulder bag. As Terry entered his hotel, Bess and George pulled up alongside her.

"Lucky you!" Bess called out.

"He's charming," George teased. "I'm sending an application to Keystone University!"

"Stop it, girls," Nancy pleaded, then added with a grin, "But he *is* handsome, isn't he?"

Without waiting for a reply, she started her car, waving good-by to Bess and George. Nancy threaded her way through the heavy traffic.

When she arrived home, her father and the housekeeper, Hannah Gruen, greeted her at the door. Mrs. Gruen had taken care of the home and reared Nancy since Mrs. Drew's death many years before. After kissing them both, Nancy led the way into the attractive, comfortable living room.

Carson Drew said with a chuckle, "Nancy, from the grip you have on that purse, you must have brought a treasure from New York."

"It may lead to one," his daughter declared.

She showed him the half-key, asking if he had ever seen anything like it.

"No."

"Dad, do you know a Terence Scott?"

"I just met him this morning. He was at my office. What made you ask?"

"This key is his. He met me at the plane."

Mr. Drew's eyes widened. "I did tell him you were arriving by plane, but I had no idea—"

"How much do you know about him?"

"Practically nothing."

"Dad, please phone Keystone University and ask what he teaches and what they think of him?"

"Gladly, Detective Drew." Her father smiled.

Nancy gave him a hug. "Oh, Dad, there's so much to tell—"

"But not now, please," said Hannah Gruen. "I've been saving dinner for you, and if you don't sit down soon, it'll be ruined."

"Dinner!" cried Nancy. "That's a lovely idea. I'll be ready in two jiffs."

She hurried upstairs. Before she even smoothed her hair, Nancy took the key from her purse and hid it among scarfs and handkerchiefs in a drawer of her dressing table.

During dinner Nancy told about her weekend and the exciting events that had taken place at the airport.

Mr. Drew said that he knew the elderly Dr. Pitt with whom Terry Scott claimed to have been in Mexico. "I'll call Keystone now."

After a slight delay, Mr. Drew was connected with the president's home, and presented his questions. In a few minutes the conversation was over.

"The report is, Nancy, that Terence Scott is an outstanding young professor, who has a leave of absence this year. He went to Mexico last summer on an exploring expedition."

"Then his story is true!" Nancy exclaimed. "Dad, is there any reason why I shouldn't help him on the case?"

"I can't give my answer to that question until I make a further investigation." Mr. Drew could not be dissuaded from this decision.

Nancy retired, still trying to account for the strange happenings of the day. But her head was hardly upon the pillow, before she fell fast asleep.

It was past midnight when she awoke with a start. The light on her bedside table was on. Hannah Gruen was gently shaking her. The woman's face was drawn and white.

"What's the matter?" Nancy asked in alarm.

The housekeeper put a finger to her lips, then whispered, "Burglar!" She signaled Nancy to put on a robe and follow her into the hall.

Mr. Drew was on the stairs. In his hand he held a golf club ready to use as a weapon.

"Hannah," he ordered, "stay close to Nancy. You two look around the rooms up here. I'm going downstairs. Yell if you find anyone."

She and Nancy looked through each room, searching closets and peering under beds. Everything seemed to be normal.

"Dad's calling us," Nancy said a few minutes later.

They hurried downstairs. Mr. Drew was in the living room, looking at the open window next to the piano.

"It's been jimmied," he said.

"Do you suppose somebody's still in the house?" Mrs. Gruen asked.

"I think that whoever it was got away," Carson Drew concluded, pointing outside the window. In the soft earth close to a rosebush, they saw a man's footprints.

"Has anything been stolen?" the housekeeper asked.

"No. I checked," Mr. Drew said.

"The black key!" thought Nancy.

She turned and raced upstairs. The key was where she had put it.

"I'm glad I didn't leave it downstairs," she told herself with a sigh of relief.

Every place that had not been searched before was investigated, in case the intruder had an accomplice hiding in the house. But there was no stranger on the premises.

"It's too bad Togo wasn't here, Nancy," Hannah said. "He would have taken care of the burglar!"

Togo, Nancy's terrier, was with Mr. Drew's sister, who was spending a three-weeks' vacation at her summer home.

When Nancy came downstairs at nine o'clock the next morning, she found Bess Marvin waiting for her. Bess sat at the table and chatted excitedly while Nancy ate breakfast.

"Mrs. Gruen told me all about last night," Bess began. "If you take Terry Scott's case, something awful is bound to happen."

Nancy raised her eyebrows. "But what?"

"Well, it seems so dangerous. And Ned Nickerson won't like it a bit. He'll be so worried, Nancy, especially when he takes a look at your professor!"

"Bess!" exclaimed Nancy, smiling. "Ned won't think anything of the sort!"

As she finished a glass of milk, the telephone rang. "Nancy, it's for you," Hannah announced.

The caller was Terry Scott. His voice sounded hoarse and excited. "Is everything all right?" he asked.

"Oh yes. Quite safe," she assured him, thinking he meant the key. "Has something happened?"

"Yes. Something serious. When I came up to my hotel room last night, a visitor was waiting for me in the closet. He struck me on the head and I didn't come to until six o'clock this morning."

"How dreadful!" Nancy gasped. "What did he look like?"

"I don't know. All I saw was a mask."

"Did he steal anything?"

"He certainly did. Took most of my notes on that Mexican expedition. I planned to use them for a lecture I'm giving soon."

"Did he take anything else?"

"Apparently not. He did a thorough search job, though, on my suitcase. Dumped everything on the floor."

Terry decided he had better say no more on the telephone. "I'll come over later and talk to you," he suggested.

"All right. I'll be here."

When Nancy told Bess what had happened, the girl's eyes grew wide with fear. "Maybe he's the same thief who came to your house last night," she said.

"I've thought of that. I ought to tell Dad," Nancy added, going to the telephone. As she started to dial, Carson Drew himself walked down the stairs.

"Good morning, girls," he said.

"Dad!" Nancy exclaimed as the lawyer bent down to kiss her cheek. "I thought you'd gone to the office."

"Not this morning," Mr. Drew replied, smiling. "I have news for you."

"I have news, too," she said, and related what Terry Scott had told her over the telephone.

"Too bad," the lawyer remarked.

"Now tell us your news," Nancy urged him.

"It's about the same young man," her father explained. "What you have just told me complicates matters still more. You recall that I hinted to you on the phone just before you left New

York about doing a little detective work for me?"

"Yes, Dad."

Before he could continue, they heard a car enter the driveway. A taxicab pulled up.

"My news will have to wait," he said.

Nancy hurried into the hall. "It's Terry Scott," she called, and opened the door.

The pale young man, a bandage on his head, entered the living room and smiled wryly. "Good morning," he said. "I'm afraid I don't look very presentable."

"Oh, it was dreadful, that man assaulting you," Bess spoke up.

"Sorry to hear it," added Mr. Drew. "Any clue to your attacker?"

"No," Terry replied. "The hotel detective and the police checked my room."

"Any idea who the man was?" Nancy asked.

Terry shrugged. "If Juarez Tino hadn't gone to Florida, I'd suspect him. But I can't think of anyone else."

Bess decided to change the subject to something more pleasant. "Terry, do you speak any of the Mexican languages?" she asked.

"Why, yes, I do. Spanish, and a couple of Indian dialects. That's one of the reasons Dr. Pitt and the others chose me to go to Mexico."

"Nancy says you almost found a fortune down there," Bess said. "What was it?"

Terry smiled. "I suspect the treasure will be one or more frogs."

"Frogs?" cried the two girls together.

The young professor nodded. "In certain ancient civilizations the frog was sacred, just as the cow is sacred in many parts of India today. Because of its religious meaning, the frog symbol was used frequently by craftsmen.

"Many of these frogs were made of silver, some of them inlaid with precious stones. A collection of such jeweled pieces would be worth a fortune."

"How did you learn about the—the frogs?" Bess asked.

"An ancient monument in Mexico carries a message in an unknown language," Terry answered. "It's all in pictures. The Indians call it the Mystery Stone, and say it tells where a fabulous treasure is buried. It is called the Frog Treasure, and according to legend, it is locked away in silver by three 'magic' obsidian keys."

"And I have half of one?" Nancy asked.

Terry nodded. "I'm hoping against hope that the treasure can't be unlocked without this missing piece, even if someone else locates the place."

"Please tell the whole story from the beginning," Bess begged. "Couldn't any Mexicans read the Mystery Stone?"

"No. They knew only the legend. Late one afternoon Dr. Pitt and I dug up a small stone tablet—the one I told you about, Nancy. From photographs we had of the Mystery Stone monument, we saw that one side of the tablet had the same picture writing as the monument.

"On the reverse side of the tablet, the ciphers had been translated into one of the ancient Indian dialects, which I know. With the help of the tablet we could solve the mystery! But, as you know, the tablet vanished."

"What about the three keys? Where did you find them?" Nancy asked.

"They were on a silver ring. This was fastened to the tablet through a hole bored in one end of it. I knew at once that they were the 'magic' keys of the legend."

"But the cipher stone was stolen—and the keys with it!" Bess exclaimed.

"And what's more important, Dr. Pitt vanished at the same time. It's his fate that's worrying me more than anything else. This morning I began to wonder if there might be some superstition about the Frog Treasure which the natives fear and are afraid that we will discover. This might be a reason for holding the doctor."

"Have you any idea what the superstition might be?" Nancy asked.

From an inner pocket Terry Scott pulled out a crude drawing. "I found this in Dr. Pitt's tent the next morning," he said.

There were actually three drawings which formed a triangle: at the lower left, a frog; at the right, what appeared to be the prostrate figure of a man; and at the top, a symbol representing the sun.

"What do they mean?" Bess asked.

Terry said he had not figured it out. But he was sure the riddle could be solved and Professor Pitt found.

"You see why I need the services of a good lawyer, Mr. Drew," he said, "and also the help of a good detective like your daughter. Can't we start work at once?"

Carson Drew was thoughtful a moment. "It looks as if solving this mystery will have to be done in Mexico," he mused.

Turning to his daughter, he said, "I'm afraid, Nancy dear, that in this case you've started something you can't finish at this time—unless you go to Mexico. I can't spare you as far away from home as that, and besides, I have some work of my own for you to do in the next few days."

CHAPTER IV

Suspicion

NANCY looked at her father in surprise, but did not argue the point. She knew he would not have asked her to turn down Terry Scott's case without good reason.

The young man showed his disappointment, but smiled politely. "Well, you can't blame me for trying, sir," he said, getting up from his chair. "Your daughter seemed to be the very person I needed to help me."

Nancy gave the mysterious drawing a last-minute look. "Have the other professors any idea what these signs mean?" she asked.

"No, none," Terry replied. "Well, I guess I'd better get back to my hotel."

"I must go, too," Bess added, rising.

After saying good-by to the callers, Nancy followed her father upstairs to his study.

"Dad, if I can't work on Terry's case," she said, "shouldn't I give back the half-key?"

The lawyer smiled quizzically. "That depends on something. I know one thing Terry Scott may or may not know. And that's why I asked you not to continue trying to solve the mystery until certain things can be proved."

Her father explained that Joshua Pitt's will left everything he owned to Terry Scott, and it was a sizable sum of money.

"Dad! How did you learn that?"

"Because," he replied, "I drew up the will. Dr. Pitt and I have a mutual friend who recommended me to him last year."

Nancy was astounded. Instantly she guessed what was in her father's mind. There was a chance Terry's whole story was a fake. The truth might be very ugly. For some reason best known to Terry, Dr. Pitt might never return and the young man would inherit the money!

"Oh, Dad, I just can't believe Terry's that kind of person," she declared.

"He probably isn't," her father said. "But it's something to keep in mind."

Nancy nodded. "Why did he come to you for help, Dad?"

"Terry quoted old Pitt as saying, 'If you're ever in trouble, go to Carson Drew. He'll get you out of it if anybody can.'"

"And you would," Nancy remarked loyally.

Her father made a mock bow. "Don't misunderstand. I like Terry, too. But my first interest is to protect Dr. Pitt. That's why I want you to take on a little investigative job."

Nancy leaned forward expectantly.

"I want you to go and see the other members of the team—Dr. Graham and Dr. Anderson," Mr. Drew proposed. "Find out what you can about the expedition, and what they think of Terry."

Nancy was eager to begin her work. "I'll start with Dr. Graham. Terry says he's at Jonsonburg College. Maybe George will drive over there with me this afternoon."

Nancy telephoned Dr. Graham's office to arrange an appointment. Next, she asked George to accompany her.

"Hypers, Nancy, I don't know how to talk to a doctor of archaeology! But I'll go."

A few minutes before three fifteen George and Nancy knocked at a door marked *Professor Graham*. A small, stooped man with wrinkled, leathery cheeks opened the door. He eyed the two girls briefly. When Nancy introduced herself and George, the professor looked at his watch.

"I see you're punctual, Miss Drew. I like young people to be on time." He stepped back from the door and invited them in.

Nancy told Dr. Graham that she was acquainted with Terry Scott, and through him had learned of the expedition to Mexico and the disappearance of Dr. Pitt.

"My father is a friend of Dr. Pitt and is much concerned about him," Nancy added. "He suggested that I come and talk to you."

The little man fixed his sharp, calculating eyes on the girl. "I suppose young Scott told you *he* found the cipher stone," the professor remarked coldly, ignoring the reference to Dr. Pitt.

"No," Nancy replied. "He said, 'Dr. Pitt and I.' Terry has a very high respect for your work, too, Professor," she added hastily.

She could see the old man relax under this compliment. "Humph! He's an arrogant young fellow. But he has a good mind. I suppose you want my opinion of the case."

Nancy nodded.

"About Pitt, now." Dr. Graham leaned back in his chair. "I don't mind saying his disappearance hardly surprised me. I like Pitt, but he's secretive. He'll listen; he'll find out what others have on their minds, but he'll never tell what he has found out."

"Do you believe, Dr. Graham," Nancy spoke up, "that Dr. Pitt went off by himself to find the treasure?"

Graham shrugged. "It's possible. Then he added, a half-smile on his face, "Some of us scientists are a bit selfish, not in acquiring money, but we want recognition; we want to discover things

"Where do you think the lost keys are?"
Nancy asked the professor

for ourselves. We're not always generous when we work together."

"But I'll give credit where credit is due," he added testily. "Terry Scott found that half-key and I agreed to let him take charge of it."

"Where do you think the lost keys are?" Nancy asked.

The professor said he was working on an idea. He did not care to reveal it then. "But Terry will never be able to solve the mystery alone."

"Have you any theories about the drawing he found in Dr. Pitt's tent?" Nancy asked.

Dr. Graham compressed his lips and shrugged. Did he know something he was not telling? Or was he too proud to admit that he could not explain the secret message?

Nancy knew it would be difficult to find out whether or not he had any suspicion about Terry in connection with Dr. Pitt's disappearance. At last she broached the subject. Dr. Graham stood up dramatically and pounded his desk.

"The idea!" he stormed when he got the full import of her question. "Maybe we four did have our differences about what we ought to do on that expedition, but I want to tell you this: not one of us would harm another for all the treasure in Mexico!"

"That's just what I wanted to hear," Nancy said, rising. "Thank you for letting me come."

Much relieved, she and George left Dr. Graham's office. On the way home, George suggested with a sly grin, "Ned will be surprised when he learns about your interest in professors. When are you seeing him again?"

Nancy grinned back. "This weekend."

After supper that evening Ned Nickerson telephoned from his fraternity house at Emerson College.

"You're not forgetting our date this weekend?" he asked anxiously.

"Of course I haven't forgotten," Nancy assured him. "I've a marvelous memory for dates—especially when they're for house parties. Bess and George are just sunk because they couldn't accept Burt's and Dave's invitations."

"Yes, it's too bad. Nancy, I have a favor to ask of you. There's a professor visiting River Heights —a fraternity brother of mine. He needs a lift to Emerson."

Nancy laughed. "Why, Ned, are you asking me to drive over with another man?"

Ned snorted. "That stuffy codger? He's probably sixty if he's a day. He's due to give a lecture here, and you know those weekend trains. I thought you wouldn't mind bringing him with you Friday."

"Glad to. Where's he staying?"

"At the Claymore Hotel. The professor's name is Terence Scott."

CHAPTER V

The Highway Trap

TERRY!

Nancy gasped in surprise and amusement.

"What's the matter?" As she hesitated in her reply, Ned asked, "You're not backing down, are you?"

"Oh no," Nancy assured him. She was tempted to reveal Terry's age but decided the joke was too good to spoil. "I'm sure Professor Scott will be very pleasant company," she added. "See you Friday, Ned. Good-by now!"

Immediately Nancy telephoned Terry and told him about Ned's call. The young professor laughed heartily at the joke. He said he would be delighted to drive to Emerson with her on Friday.

Nancy now spoke of the obsidian half-key, saying that perhaps she should bring it along. Terry begged her to keep it.

"I haven't given up hope you'll agree to help me solve the mystery," he said.

After she had hung up, Mr. Drew confided to Nancy that he was fast losing any suspicion he might have had regarding Terry. But there were still points about Dr. Pitt's disappearance which needed explaining.

"Maybe I'll learn more over the weekend," Nancy said hopefully. "I'll call on Dr. Anderson. He's not far from Emerson."

On Thursday Nancy busied herself with preparations for the weekend party. The next day proved to be a warm, sunny day, so Nancy decided to put down the top of her convertible. Promptly at eleven o'clock she pulled up in front of the Claymore Hotel. Terry was waiting.

Soon they were rolling along the wide highway toward Emerson College. It was not long before they found themselves once more discussing the mystery in Mexico.

"You've never told me much about Juarez Tino," Nancy said.

"That's rather a long story," Terry answered. "Mind if I tell it while we have lunch? I'm starved."

Nancy parked at an attractive roadside restaurant, near the brow of a hill, and they found a secluded table.

"I disliked Juarez Tino," Terry told her, "the

first day I saw him. He was a shifty sort of fellow. According to his story, he was exploring a neighboring site. But he was always coming over to see what we were doing.

"He asked hundreds of questions, and prowled around our excavation ditches after dark to see if we'd left anything around. I was sure he was up to some deviltry."

"Did the other professors distrust him, too?"

"They didn't suspect him in the same way I did. Dr. Pitt told me to ignore the fellow. I didn't agree. It seemed to me that if we let Juarez hang around, sooner or later we'd have trouble on our hands."

"Did you?"

"One day I lost my temper. I told Juarez to keep out of our excavation. We had a regular setto, and the upshot was that I ran him off the place."

"Did you find out anything about him?"

"Nothing very conclusive. He'd taken a few courses somewhere and had a smattering of this and that. His specialty was supposed to be ancient gems. But his reputation wasn't good. There were rumors that he'd once tried to pass off some fake pieces."

Nancy asked if Juarez had ever come back after he was chased away.

"Yes. Although he stayed out of my sight, he did plenty of snooping when he thought I wasn't around. Once in a while I would get a glimpse of his wife."

"What was she like?"

The young man frowned. "You wouldn't like her, Nancy. She wears loud clothes and always makes herself conspicuous. She has a bold manner, and her voice is harsh. In fact, her whole personality suggested just one thing to me—cruelty."

Nancy thought, "This couple sounds equal to taking on almost any underhanded work!"

As she and Terry stepped outdoors into the sunshine, she was not thinking of the dinner party at Emerson. She was wondering about Mrs. Juarez Tino and her husband. If Professor Pitt were in their clutches, he was not being treated well, she felt sure.

Nancy was about to step into her car when Terry touched her arm. "Look!" he said in a low, tense voice. "Those two men up the hill—I think they're spying on us."

When Nancy turned her head to look, the pair, with hats pulled low over their faces, stepped hurriedly into a black sedan. The car quickly got under way and passed out of sight over the top of the hill.

"Those men ran the minute we looked at them," Terry said. "I wonder why they did that."

"Did you recognize them?" Nancy asked.

"No."

"We'll watch out for them, just the same," Nancy decided.

"I'll feel better when we get to Emerson," Terry replied a bit nervously. "Perhaps you'd better speed up."

Nancy shook off her somber mood and grinned mischievously. "Do you suppose your elderly nerves can stand the strain, Professor?"

"Give them a try!"

They stepped into her car and she started it rolling once more toward Emerson. The speedometer crept steadily higher, but Nancy did not overtake the two sinister-looking strangers in the black car. Finally she and Terry began to enjoy the flying landscape, the swift rush of wind, the dips and curves of the road.

Then suddenly—too late—they saw disaster just ahead. They had rounded a bend. Beyond was a wide repair ditch. Desperately Nancy wrenched the wheel to the left.

But she could not make it in time. There was a hurtling impact as the car nose-dived into the ditch! Nancy blacked out.

CHAPTER VI

New Challenge

WHEN Nancy regained consciousness a few minutes later, Terry Scott was bending over her.

"Nancy!" he whispered anxiously.

"I'm all right," she managed to say, but her head ached badly. "You're not hurt?"

"A few bruises. But we're lucky."

The couple got out and surveyed the car. It was tilted precariously on its front end.

"There should have been a warning sign," Nancy said grimly.

Terry pointed. "There was a sign—but not where it should have been."

Lying at the side of the ditch was a long board. " 'Danger. Road Repairs. Drive Slowly,' " he read aloud. "A lot of good that does us now! The road gang shouldn't have been so careless."

"Don't blame the road gang," Nancy said. "I

believe that sign was deliberately removed just before we got here."

"Nancy, that would be murder!"

"It very nearly was murder," she answered. "And by those two men who were watching us at the restaurant, I'll bet."

Terry dragged the sign around the bend to warn other motorists. He had just returned to Nancy when they heard the squeal of brakes.

Nancy and Terry relaxed as they saw a kindly-looking, middle-aged couple in the car that came around the bend.

"Oh, my dears!" the woman cried, getting out of the car. "Is anyone—"

Terry said no one else was involved in the accident. Nancy added that they were all right except she had a headache.

The man offered the young people a ride, but Nancy preferred waiting until a wrecker could come. The friendly strangers promised to stop at the next town and send back mechanics, as well as a state trooper.

A few minutes later a tow truck arrived and two men in overalls stepped out. In a short time they had Nancy's car on the road and were checking it for damage.

Both mechanics grinned. "Some car!" one commented. "She's got a few dents and scratches. But no real harm done by her tumble. No reason why you two can't keep goin' under your own power.

'Course, you'd better check again when you get where you're goin'."

As the men were leaving, a state trooper rode up on a motorcycle. Nancy and Terry told him their story. He said that a watch would be set for the two men whom the young people thought were responsible for the removal of the road sign.

Then Nancy and Terry started off once more for Emerson. Terry took the wheel.

"You relax and pamper that head of yours," he told Nancy, "or you won't be able to show up at the dance tomorrow. I'm counting on at least one dance with you, young lady."

"Are you going?" Nancy asked in surprise.

"Well, that depends on whether or not I get an invitation."

"I'll be looking for you," Nancy said.

When they reached Emerson College, Terry got off at the president's home, where he had been invited to stay. Nancy drove on to meet Ned Nickerson at the Chi Omega Epsilon fraternity house.

Tall, athletic Ned saw Nancy drive up and ran out to greet her. When he noticed the dents in the car, he gasped, "What happened? Were you in an accident?"

When she told what had occurred, Ned's tanned face took on a look of deep concern. He insisted she call Hannah to say she had arrived at Emerson. Then he drove Nancy to the college infirmary for a checkup. To his relief she was pronounced all right.

On the way back to the fraternity house, Ned asked, "How did you and the prof hit it off? Was he much bother?"

Nancy smiled demurely. "He was a lamb. He even insisted on driving part of the way himself. And you know what I think you should do, Ned? Invite him to the fraternity dance. As your fraternity brother, he'd be immensely flattered."

"All right," Ned agreed reluctantly. "I'll see that he gets an invitation."

At dinner she mentioned that her father wished her to call on Dr. Anderson, a professor of geology at Clifton Institute nearby.

"It would be nice if you could drive me over," she said. "How about Sunday?"

"Look here, Nancy. Is this some more of your detective work?"

Nancy admitted that she had become interested in a fascinating mystery and would tell him more about it on the drive over. For the time being, she was just going to enjoy the house party.

Next afternoon there was a football game. It was a close contest with Harper. Emerson pulled ahead only in the last quarter to win by a score of 14 to 7.

Ned played a spectacular game as quarterback. He scored the first touchdown on a brilliant dash around the Harper end, and threw a pass to the left halfback for the winning touchdown. Nancy cheered until her voice was hoarse.

Later, when they were dancing at the fraternity house, Ned remarked that he had not seen any elderly men. "I guess Professor Scott decided not to come."

Nancy suppressed a smile. A few minutes later she saw a tall young man on the fringe of the crowd. As she and Ned reached him, Nancy stopped and said:

"Hello! I'm glad you got here. Ned, I'd like you to meet Professor Terence Scott. Terry, this is your fraternity brother Ned Nickerson."

Terry put out his hand. Ned's jaw dropped and he gave Nancy a sidewise glance. The name Scott had hit him like a delayed-action bomb.

"You're Professor Scott who's giving a lecture here tomorrow?" he exclaimed.

Terry grinned. "I guess I am, Brother Nickerson!"

Ned shot Nancy an "I'll-get-even" look, then burst out laughing. "Well, you two kept your secret well," he said.

He immediately introduced Terry to his fraternity brothers and the girls with them. Terry became popular at once.

When the dance ended, he told Nancy and Ned, "I haven't had so much fun since my own college days."

The next day, directly after lunch, Nancy and

Ned set out for Clifton Institute. Nancy kept her promise to tell Ned about the mystery of the black key, and the strange events that had taken place in connection with it.

"That's why I want to talk to Dr. Anderson," she concluded. "He may give us a clue."

They located the robust, forty-five-year-old professor seated in a garden behind one of the faculty houses. He wore comfortable tweeds and was puffing on a briar pipe.

"Never find me indoors, weather like this," he told his callers after Nancy had introduced herself and Ned.

Dr. Anderson went on to say that he felt he could teach his students more on field trips than they could possibly get out of books. "On the ninth of this coming month I'm taking a group of special students from various colleges on a field trip to Florida."

"How exciting!" exclaimed Nancy.

"Great country, Florida," the professor said. "Fascinating history."

Nancy maneuvered the conversation to Mexico, and explained that her father knew Dr. Joshua Pitt. "Dr. Anderson, do you have any theories about where Pitt might be?"

The question seemed to annoy the professor. With a frown he replied, "I'm interested in facts, not theories, Miss Drew."

He further astounded her by saying that Juarez

Tino had called on him a few weeks before. He had offered to tell where Pitt and the missing cipher tablet were if Anderson would pay him for the information.

"You didn't do it?" Nancy asked excitedly.

"That rascally scoundrel?" the professor exploded. "I should say not. I threatened to call the police, and then threw him out of my office!"

Nancy asked a few more questions, but Dr. Anderson became evasive. Realizing she could get no more information from him, she thanked him for the interview and left with Ned.

As they drove back to Emerson, Nancy remarked, "If I had been in Dr. Anderson's place, I would have tried to find out where Juarez Tino went."

Ned agreed. "Do you think he might be holding Dr. Pitt for ransom?"

"If so, there's no telling what might happen to the poor man," Nancy said. "I must find Juarez Tino just as soon as I can!"

"Sounds too dangerous," Ned retorted. "Remember, I like you all in one piece!"

"Don't worry," Nancy replied laughingly. "So do I!"

That afternoon she and Ned attended Terry Scott's lecture at the college auditorium. The young scientist thrilled his audience with a story about a Mexican jungle, where there had once lived an ancient race of people quite unlike any of their neighbors. From statues that had been found, it was thought they might have been pygmies.

"But they were people of a high culture," Terry said, "who made many beautiful objects. These are just beginning to be uncovered. I had some color pictures of them, but unfortunately all of my slides, as well as my notes, mysteriously disappeared a short time ago."

Nancy whispered to Ned that this was when Terry was assaulted at his hotel. Toward the end of the lecture, the young professor mentioned his own work in Mexico and the cipher stone.

"Someday I hope to come back here and tell you that the cipher stone has solved a great mystery," he remarked, looking straight at Nancy.

When the lecture was over, his listeners applauded loudly.

"Never heard people so enthusiastic over this kind of lecture," Ned declared as he and Nancy left the auditorium.

"Terry's really good, isn't he?" Nancy said.

The couple had dinner that evening at a popular steak house, and discussed plans for Ned's Thanksgiving vacation.

They said good night at ten, since Ned had classes the next morning and Nancy planned to start early on the drive home.

Terry drove most of the way back to River Heights on Monday. "I'm glad this trip was uneventful," he declared laughingly as he said good-by at his hotel.

"I'll be in touch soon about the mystery," Nancy promised as she waved, and headed home.

"Well, I'm glad you're back, and safe and sound," said Hannah Gruen as she met Nancy at the door.

"Any news here?" Nancy asked.

"Yes. Your father left town. Didn't say when he'd be back. And call Bess or George right away."

"Important?"

"If you could hear them, you'd think so!"

Nancy hurried to the telephone and called the Marvin house.

"At last!" Bess gasped. "Wait there. George and I will be right over."

A few minutes later the cousins arrived in the Marvin car. They joined Nancy in her bedroom where she was unpacking.

"Did you have fun?" Bess began.

George cut her short. "Let's tell Nancy our news first. She might want to report it to the police."

"Yes, please do," Nancy begged.

The girls said they might have a clue to the person or persons who had caused the car accident, about which they had already heard from Hannah.

"It all started in Cliffwood," said Bess. "Remember that terrible man who said all those awful things to you at the airport?"

"You mean Wilfred Porterly?"

"He's the one." George took up the story. "Bess and I were shopping Friday in Cliffwood when we spotted him."

The cousins were so sure he had not been telling the truth about himself at the airport that they had decided to follow him and see what they could find out.

"We trailed him to a hotel, where he went into a phone booth," George reported. "He dialed a number and talked to somebody named King."

"Conway King?" Nancy asked excitedly.

"I don't know. He just said King. But he was talking about you, Nancy. We heard him say, 'That Drew girl and Scott are acting too smart. You know what to do.' "

"Then what happened?"

"King must have answered quickly and to the point, because Porterly said, 'That sounds all right.' Then he hung up."

Bess said the girls had expected Porterly to go upstairs, and were planning what to do next, when he suddenly went out a rear exit.

"We followed him," said George, "but he disappeared. I think he caught a glimpse of us."

"The hotel clerk said nobody was registered there under the name of Porterly," Bess added.

"Was there a Mr. King listed?" Nancy asked.

"No," George replied.

"What time did Porterly make the phone call?"

"A little after ten," George declared. "It must have been, because we left home at nine."

Nancy was thoughtful. It was unfortunate that she had caught only a brief glimpse of the men's backs when they had jumped into their parked sedan near the restaurant. Had the shorter one been King—alias Juarez Tino—back from Florida? Had the taller man been Porterly?

Nancy told the girls about the two strangers who had been watching the restaurant.

"Nancy, you might have been killed!" Bess said with a shiver.

George agreed. "Those villains are plotting trouble for you as well as for Terry. Since one plan didn't work, they'll try another."

All the time Nancy was relating details about the house party, her mind dwelled on George's remark.

"I ought to warn Terry!" Nancy decided after the cousins left to return home.

She hurried into her father's study and telephoned. Nancy quickly related the story and her suspicions.

Terry whistled in surprise. "Well, that clears up the mystery of the road sign," he remarked.

"When they find their scheme didn't work," Nancy said, "they'll try something else. Terry, you're the one they're really after. I think you should leave town for a few days."

"Oh, I'll be all right," the young professor replied reassuringly. "But how about you? Does your father know what happened?"

Nancy told him her father was away for an indefinite stay.

"That settles it," Terry said. "You and Mrs. Gruen should not be in that house tonight. Stay at some hotel."

"Nonsense," Nancy told him. "We'll be perfectly safe, especially if Juarez Tino thinks I'm scared off the case. But why do you have to stay in River Heights?"

"I have no choice. You know I'm a bit of a linguist. A woman here engaged me just this afternoon to translate an old diary for her, and I've accepted. It belonged to her grandfather, a sea captain. It's sort of a puzzle and she has persuaded me to decipher it for her."

"Can't you do your translating somewhere else, while you're in hiding?" Nancy asked.

Terry said the woman considered the diary a priceless relic and would not permit it out of her sight. That meant he would have to work on it at her home in River Heights.

"But here's an idea," he said. "She and her husband have invited me to stay with them while I'm doing the work."

"Well, that might be safer than staying at the hotel," Nancy said. "I'd suggest you go there immediately. But please do it quietly. Don't let Juarez Tino or Porterly know where you are!"

"All right," Terry agreed. "If you want to get in touch with me, I'll be at the Earl Wangells'. They're in the phone book."

A sudden look of alarm came into Nancy's eyes. "Terry, did you say the Wangells? On Fairview Avenue?"

"Yes. Do you know them?"

Nancy's voice was excited now. "Terry, listen to me. I beg you, don't go there and stay. Don't even take the job!"

Terry was astounded. "Why not?" he asked.

"I can't tell you over the phone. But Dad would say the same thing if he were here. Please don't go there, Terry."

For a minute he did not reply. When he did speak, the young man's voice was kindly but determined.

"Thanks for warning me. But I've just got to run the risk. I must see that diary again," he said. "I believe it will help solve the mystery of the black keys."

CHAPTER VII

A Mysterious Diary

VARIOUS thoughts raced through Nancy's mind. Her father distrusted the Wangells. Why had they contacted Terry? And why did he think the diary would aid in solving the mystery of the black keys?

"Please," she said, "let's talk about this some more before you go to the Wangells' again. But not on the phone. I'm having dinner at George Fayne's. Could you come there afterward?"

Terry agreed. At eight o'clock he arrived. After she had introduced him to George's parents, the Faynes went off to watch a television program in the recreation room.

"The first thing I want to know," the young professor said, once he was seated, "is why you distrust the Wangells."

Nancy explained that several years before, the

Wangells had done some traveling in Europe. "When they came back, they set themselves up as experts on rare, old pictures."

"Fake art dealers?" Terry suggested.

"Yes. They convinced a widow that they had some rare French paintings. She paid a fancy price for them, only to discover later that the pictures were worthless."

"Did she sue?" Terry asked.

"Yes. But the Wangells claimed they had bought the pictures from a young man named DuPlaine, and had been duped themselves—that DuPlaine had painted the pictures and forged a famous artist's signature."

"How did you hear of the case?" Terry wanted to know.

"A friend of Dad's defended DuPlaine," Nancy replied. "DuPlaine admitted he had painted the pictures but said they were only copies he had made, as a student, in the museums. He had sold them as copies for practically nothing."

"What was the Wangells' answer to that?"

"They acted injured and indignant. Mr. Wangell had a bill of sale and all sorts of documents to prove they had paid a high price."

Terry asked how the case had been settled. Nancy said the court had decided there was insufficient evidence, and had dismissed the case.

"But my father always believed that the Wangells had forged the bill of sale, the documents, and the signatures on the paintings."

"Nice people," Terry commented.

"You see why I'm convinced they're up to something dishonest in this diary business," Nancy said. "It seems odd that Mrs. Wangell won't let you borrow it."

"She says she can't run the risk of losing it," Terry replied.

"I wonder if that's the real reason," Nancy mused. "And by the way, you haven't told me what Mrs. Wangell's diary has to do with the mystery of the black keys."

"From skimming through it, I gather it is full of unpublished legends which I suspect may have some bearing on our case."

"How?"

"Mrs. Wangell's sea-captain grandfather retired in Florida, but he'd picked up stories everywhere, especially in Mexico."

"I see why you want to read the diary." Nancy smiled. "But I still don't like your dealing with the Wangells. Promise you won't stay there. How about going to a small hotel tonight and sending for your baggage so no one will know where you are?"

"I'd like to please you," Terry replied, "and be safe besides." He grinned. "I'll go to the Parkview and ask a porter to take my things over there. Ever since that attack, I've kept everything locked in my bags, so the move will be easy."

"I believe we ought to check the story of Mrs. Wangell's grandfather being a sea captain, and the valuable diary belonging to him," Nancy said.

Terry lifted his eyebrows. "I never thought of that. It's a good idea."

Nancy and Terry went to the recreation room and Nancy thanked the Faynes for dinner. "I'm sorry I haven't been the least bit sociable since dinner. And now you'll think me rude, but would you mind terribly if Terry and I go? I want to stop at Mrs. Prescott's on the way home."

George groaned. "Hypers, Nancy, don't you ever take time out from a mystery?"

Nancy shook her head laughingly as she and Terry said good-by.

While driving to Mrs. Prescott's, Nancy explained that the woman's business was tracing family trees.

"She has studied the history of every family in this area, and is president of the local historical society. She has stacks of records."

Mrs. Prescott was at home and welcomed her two guests at once into the library. She seemed delighted to have Nancy ask a question on her favorite subject.

"Mrs. Wangell? Let me see," she mused, squeezing her pince-nez onto her nose. "She was Lillian Webster before she married."

The woman's eyes studied the shelves. "This will take a little while, my dear. Do you mind waiting?"

"Not at all," Nancy replied.

At last Mrs. Prescott turned away from her books and records, and took off her glasses.

"I have checked both of Mrs. Wangell's grandfathers," she said, "and neither of them was a sea captain."

Nancy and Terry pretended surprise.

"It's all in the record," Mrs. Prescott insisted. "Neither of them followed the sea at any time."

"I guess I have the story confused," Nancy murmured.

She thanked Mrs. Prescott for her help and hurried out to the car with Terry.

"You see, Mrs. Wangell isn't to be trusted," Nancy said. "I think you should insist upon taking that diary to the hotel and translating it before she becomes suspicious and changes her mind."

"She'll never agree to my taking it," Terry objected.

Nancy thought a moment. Suddenly she remembered a small camera her father had presented her on her latest birthday. She kept it in the glove compartment of the car. Now she took it out and gave it to Terry.

"Put this in your pocket and take it to the Wangells' tomorrow. The camera's loaded with self-developing film. Ask to borrow the diary, and if Mrs. Wangell refuses, take pictures of the pages you think may be especially important."

Terry promised to do as she suggested. Then, making sure they were not being followed, Nancy drove him to his new hotel, the Parkview.

"Sure you'll be all right?" he asked. "I hate to think of your spending the night in that big house without your father."

"Nonsense! I'm not the least bit worried," Nancy said with a laugh.

Though Nancy was not alarmed over the situation, it was quite apparent, when she reached home, that Hannah Gruen was. The faithful housekeeper was waiting at the front door.

"Thank goodness you're back!" she exclaimed.

Nancy put an affectionate hand on the woman's shoulder. "You're a lamb to be so concerned. But here I am, safe and sound. And maybe tomorrow Dad will come home."

Nancy went up to her room, undressed, and slid into bed. As she dropped off to sleep, she could hear Hannah still busy in the kitchen. "What a clatter!" Nancy thought in amusement.

When she awoke, it was in bewildered alarm. Somewhere in the darkened house there was loud banging and jangling. Simultaneously, something crashed heavily and there was the thud of foot-steps.

Springing out of bed, Nancy pulled on a robe

and rushed into the hall. There was no further sound. The entire house was in darkness.

Her first thought was of Hannah Gruen. She stepped quickly into the housekeeper's bedroom and flicked on the light. The room was empty, the bed not turned down.

Suddenly Nancy heard a moan from the floor below. She dashed to the head of the stairs and turned on the lower hall light.

Close to the front door lay Hannah Gruen!

CHAPTER VIII

A Lesson in Sleuthing

NEAR Mrs. Gruen's right hand was a rolling pin. Evidently she had dropped it. Stretched across the hall between chairs was a homemade burglar alarm—clothesline strung with tin pans and kitchen utensils. Nancy ran down the stairs.

"Hannah!" she cried, bending over the housekeeper. "What happened?"

The dazed woman opened her eyes and whispered, "Get him! Get him!"

Nancy looked out the hall window but saw no one. She helped the housekeeper to a sofa, then raced through the first floor, peering into closets and behind doors. There was no sign of any disturbance except in the hall. Evidently the burglar alarm had scared off the intruder.

Nancy notified the police. Then she hurried back to Hannah.

"Shall I call a doctor?" she asked anxiously.

61

The woman shook her head. "All I've got are bruises—and a bump on my head."

"Did he hit you with something?"

"No. I heard him trying to open the front door lock, so I waited in the dark. I thought if he got in, he'd run into that line, and I'd nab him. But I wasn't quick enough. When he hit those pans, one of them caught me on the head and dazed me a bit. That's why I didn't see where he went."

Nancy brought a washcloth wrung out in ice water and bathed Mrs. Gruen's swollen forehead.

"My, that feels good," the housekeeper said.

Nancy asked why the strange burglar alarm had been put up.

"I had an idea someone might visit us," the woman confessed. "I rigged an alarm at each door and window on the first floor."

Nancy slipped into the hall to remove Hannah's alarm system. Her eye caught a small sheet of paper lying just inside the front door and she picked it up. Printed boldly in pencil was a warning message. It read:

NO MORE INTERFERENCE OR THERE WILL BE
TROUBLE FOR YOU

"What are you doing?" Hannah asked.

Nancy returned to the living room and read the message aloud. She remarked that the note might have been written by Juarez Tino. Not wishing to alarm the housekeeper, however, she added quickly, "It may not be for you or me. Dad makes enemies in his legal work, you know. Some crank could have written it."

Hannah started to speak, but Nancy patted her arm and continued, "You were a darling—and brave, too—to rig up that burglar alarm and lie in wait. You almost caught him!"

Just then the shriek of brakes and tramping footsteps told her that the police had arrived. Nancy ushered Sergeant Malloy and two of his men into the hall, explaining what had happened. She showed them the note.

While the police busied themselves taking footprints and fingerprints, Nancy decided to look outside. Taking her pocket flashlight, she went to the porch and peered over the railing.

The beam of her light revealed two slips of paper caught in a barberry bush. Undoubtedly the intruder had dropped them. Excitedly Nancy examined them. One contained the number 74772. On the other was printed "5 x 7 and one."

Nancy returned to the hall and copied the notations, then handed the slips to the police.

"I'll work on them. They're a good clue," Sergeant Malloy said.

When the officers had concluded their investigation, the sergeant told Nancy and Hannah he would send a plainclothesman to watch the house.

After the police left, Hannah and Nancy returned to bed for a few more hours of sleep. The following morning Nancy was awakened by the ringing of the telephone. She was delighted when she recognized the deep voice of her father.

"How's everything?" he asked.

When Nancy told him what had happened during the night, Carson Drew expressed concern.

"My plane will get in this afternoon," he said. "In the meantime, I advise you not to go out of the house alone. And look after Hannah. That experience must have been a severe shock to her."

Nancy promised to do as he suggested, and as soon as she had dressed, insisted upon preparing breakfast alone.

Hannah protested at first, but at last gratefully sat down to read the morning paper. After eating, Nancy tidied the dining room and kitchen. She was just putting away the last plate when Bess Marvin popped into the kitchen.

"I can't believe my eyes! You in that apron— and Hannah sitting on the sun porch reading at nine o'clock in the morning!"

Nancy grinned. "Did she tell you about the excitement last night?"

"Yes," Bess said. "And you know what I think? You ought to have a bodyguard."

Leading her friend to a window, Nancy pointed out a slender man in a gray suit and a soft hat walking near the driveway entrance.

"One of the plainclothesmen the police sent. It makes me feel very important."

Bess giggled. "As if you were an heiress with a pile of diamonds in your bureau drawer."

"It's a black key, instead," Nancy countered. "And only half of one, at that."

"When's your dad coming home?" Bess asked. When she heard he would arrive that afternoon, she added, "That's good news. You should celebrate. I'll help you get dinner. Let me make a pie."

Shortly before noon Bess was in the kitchen beating up the meringue for a mountainous lemon pie. Nancy was seated on a stool beside her, but she was not watching the pie making. She was studying the mysterious numbers she had found in the shrubbery the night before.

The "5 x 7 and one" completely stymied her. It suggested nothing at all. The 74772 was easier. The 7 she thought, might be a River Heights telephone exchange. Whose number could 4772 be?

Suddenly she had an idea. With an excited gasp, Nancy jumped off the stool and rushed into the hall. Quickly she thumbed through the River Heights telephone directory to the W's.

Her hunch was correct. River Heights 7–4772 was listed as the Wangells' number! She rushed back to the kitchen and told Bess.

"How on earth did you figure that out?" the plump girl gasped.

Nancy said she had wondered ever since hearing about the diary why Mrs. Wangell had picked Terry to translate it. The whole thing was clear now.

"There's some connection between the Wangells and at least one of Terry's enemies," Nancy explained.

"The one who came here last night and dropped the pieces of paper!" Bess exclaimed. "Oh, Nancy, this is awful!"

"I must warn Terry," Nancy said. "I hope he's at the Parkview."

Her heart was pounding excitedly as she telephoned the hotel.

"I was just going to call you, Nancy," Terry said. "I worked all morning on Mrs. Wangell's diary, and . . ."

"Then she let you borrow it?"

"No, but I took some pictures with your camera. The black keys we found in Mexico are mentioned in the diary!"

Nancy was so surprised at Terry's news that she forgot to mention her own discovery.

"I want to see the pictures," she cried. "Bess and I are having lunch here in half an hour. Will you join us?"

Terry thought this a splendid idea. Nancy asked him to try covering his tracks so his enemies would not know where he was going. Half an hour later he arrived.

Lunch was a merry affair, but directly afterward Nancy talked to him seriously about the scraps of paper she had found. Terry could make nothing of the "5 x 7 and one" notation.

"So your would-be burglar had the Wangells' number." The young professor whistled. "I can't stop going there now," he continued. "I'm just beginning to get some valuable facts from the diary. Wait until you see what I brought."

He opened a briefcase and laid several photographs and carbon copies of notes on the table.

"At your suggestion, Nancy," he said, "I left my notes with the diary. Mrs. Wangell doesn't know I have these copies."

"Good."

Terry said that most of the diary was a puzzle to him.

Nancy picked up several of the pictures and studied them. "Will you leave them with me for a while?" she asked. "Perhaps I can find the answer."

"I'd certainly like to have you try," Terry replied. "But here's one I did figure out," he said, handing it over.

The photograph was of page seventy-six in the diary. The upper half of the sheet was covered by handwriting. On the lower part was the rough drawing of a key. Nancy read the strange text:

"In this sodden wilderness I met a curious character, a Swamp Indian. He told me of the hiding place of Treasure, and of three Black Keys that would unlock the Secret of the Ages."

Nancy could not make out the next sentence. It seemed to be in a foreign language. When she asked Terry about it, he said it was in Indian dialect. When translated, it meant:

"If Fortune be kind, the Sun and Raindrop keys will help me find this secret myself."

Underneath the text was the faded outline of a key. Examining it carefully, Nancy could see a design on the stem. One of the symbols in the design looked like the sun. The other could symbolize rain.

"I'll get your half-key, Terry, and we'll compare them."

Nancy got the key and placed it beside the one in the photograph. The lower half of the one in the picture and the relic Terry had brought from Mexico were identical!

"Are there any other references to the black keys?" Nancy asked excitedly.

Terry nodded and picked up a page of notes he said had come from pages ninety and one hundred.

"Here is something I translated from the Spanish. It says, 'Today I heard another story about the Keys of Sun and Raindrop. Whoever finds the secret may be Ruler of Mankind,' and listen to this! 'Look for the Frog.' "

"It's the same Frog Treasure mentioned on the Mystery Stone!" Nancy exclaimed.

"It looks that way," Terry agreed.

Bess was rereading the text above the key drawing. "Where is the 'sodden wilderness'? And who is the 'Swamp Indian'?" she asked.

Terry said he wished he knew. If it were true that a sea captain owned the diary, even though he was not Mrs. Wangell's grandfather, there was no way to prove it. If a name had ever been in the book, someone had torn it out, along with several other pages.

"I suspect Mrs. Wangell did the tearing," Bess decided. "She probably didn't want to be caught lying about the diary's owner."

Terry said the rest of the notes he had made that day were interesting, but he doubted if they had any bearing on the mystery.

"Terry, it's important you go on with what you're doing. Only now, translating and deciphering the diary is just part of your job."

"What do you mean?"

"I mean you're to become a detective."

"A—what?"

Nancy bobbed her head seriously. "The Wangells are dishonest. That's been proved. They need you for translating the diary. But once you've given them what they want, you won't be safe."

Terry stared, unbelieving. Nancy went on to say that it was necessary to find out more about what they were up to, before the work on the diary was finished.

"It isn't hard to do some simple sleuthing," she said encouragingly. "You see, it's not just the big things—like the diary—that are important. If you want to solve your mystery, you should start noticing the little things, too. For instance," Nancy went on, "did you notice the mail in the hall as you came in?"

"Good grief, no! Am I supposed to?"

"Of course. Postmarks and return addresses are important clues. How about the pad on the telephone desk? Any messages?"

"That's snooping."

"I'm afraid a good detective has to snoop," Nancy said.

Suddenly the young professor remembered something. His eyes widened, and he leaned forward excitedly.

"Maybe I do notice things after all," he said.

"What?" both girls asked at once.

"This morning at the Wangells'," Terry said, "while I was in the study, Mrs. Wangell made a telephone call. I just happened to overhear part of it."

"Whom was she calling?" Nancy asked.

"I don't know. But she said, 'I won't forget. The name's King.' She laughed with sort of a sneer, and added, 'Some king he is!' Then she hung up."

"You *are* a detective, Terry!" Nancy praised the young professor. "The 'King' Mrs. Wangell mentioned must be Conway King—the name Juarez Tino uses!"

CHAPTER IX

Terry Disappears

TERRY smiled. "That seems to prove the Tinos and Mrs. Wangell are in league."

"Keep your eyes open and make sure of that," Nancy begged him. "Try to find out how the Wangells got that diary."

Later that afternoon, when Terry and Bess had gone, Nancy again studied the photographs of the drawings. When her father arrived, she put them aside and went to greet him.

"Oh, it's so good to have you back!" Nancy exclaimed, giving him a hug and a kiss. "You should see the pie Bess made to celebrate your homecoming."

Carson Drew sighed. "In that case I'll have to stay home and not leave until tomorrow."

"Leave?" Nancy cried. "But, Dad, I have so much to tell you about Terry's mystery. I saw

Dr. Anderson, and I think we've found another clue in an old diary."

She accompanied the lawyer to the living-room sofa, then proceeded with her story.

"Well, you have been busy," her father said. "Good results, too. I guess there's no reason now why you shouldn't work on Terry's case. And I have news of my own," he added.

Upon returning to his office, Mr. Drew had found a letter from a man in Baltimore. Caswell P. Breed claimed to be a cousin of the missing Dr. Pitt and demanded a share in any money he might have left.

"Dad!" Nancy exclaimed. "How did he know you're Dr. Pitt's lawyer?"

Mr. Drew said this was exactly what he intended to find out. "Since I have to go to Baltimore anyway, in connection with another case, I'll look up Breed," he said.

Nancy strongly suspected that Breed was not really Pitt's cousin, and told her father so.

"Well, real or not," he said, "I'm going to Baltimore. I'd like you to go along and help me, and also meet some friends."

"I'd love to. But first, I want to tell Terry about this Breed person. Maybe he knows him, or Dr. Pitt might have mentioned him."

Nancy quickly telephoned Terry. He was amazed to hear about the letter. The young man had never heard of Breed.

As Nancy put down the telephone, a thought struck her. "Dad," she said, "what gave Breed the idea that Dr. Pitt is dead?"

Mr. Drew looked at Nancy admiringly. "That's something I must find out."

The lawyer wired ahead for hotel reservations. After dinner he and Nancy boarded an evening plane for Baltimore. On the way Nancy told her father that plainclothesmen were watching the house.

"Just the same I brought the mysterious pictures with me, and the half-key."

"Good idea," the lawyer said.

At nine-thirty the next morning Nancy and her father taxied to a ramshackle dwelling situated next to a factory. *C. P. Breed* was inscribed on a card nailed above the knocker.

The door was opened by an old man. Mr. Drew introduced himself and Nancy, saying he was the lawyer from River Heights and would like to hear more about Mr. Breed's claim.

The man stroked his whiskered chin, and limping, led the way into the sitting room. "I'll talk to y'all," he said in a high-pitched voice, "but I won't give up the claim. Doc said not to."

Nancy glanced at her father. "When did you last see your cousin?" she asked Mr. Breed.

The old man scratched his head. "He ain't no cousin o' mine. He's my doc, an' a good one, sure enough. Fixed my broken leg what I got at the factory. An' he told me not to give up my claim to any o' you lawyers."

"There must be some mistake," Mr. Drew said. He took the letter from his pocket and handed it to the old man. "Did you write this?"

Mr. Breed pulled a pair of spectacles from his vest pocket, adjusted them on his nose, and peered at the letter.

"This is me an' it ain't me," he said. "Breed's my name, but I don't know Dr. Pitt an' I ain't his cousin, an' I didn't write this."

"Do you know who could have sent it?" Nancy asked.

The man said he did not have the slightest idea, adding testily, "But I'd like to get hold o' the person who used my name!"

As his callers rose to leave, he accompanied them to the door.

On a hunch Nancy asked him if he knew any people named Scott, Graham, Anderson, Tino, King, Porterly, and Wangell. The answer was No in each case.

"You didn't leave out one," the lawyer teased his daughter as they rode off. "But I know what's in your mind; that one of them wanted to work some scheme while we were away, and sent that letter to get us out of town. Which one do you suspect?"

"Juarez Tino," Nancy replied quickly. "I'm sure he's the ringleader of that group. We'd better phone home and see if anything has happened."

"You take over while I go to the courthouse," Mr. Drew suggested.

For the next three hours Nancy kept busy at the hotel. First she telephoned Hannah Gruen to be sure everything was all right.

"Yes," the housekeeper replied. "Now stop worrying, honey."

"Be extra careful," Nancy warned, and told Mrs. Gruen about the fake letter.

Nancy next turned her attention to the photographs Terry had made of the diary pages. There were nine of them, and not one of the strange drawings suggested a picture.

Then Nancy had an idea. She bought a pad of thin tracing paper, and cut nine sheets to the exact dimensions of the photographs. On each sheet she made a careful tracing of one of the drawings, using India ink.

Laying aside the original photographs, Nancy began to juggle the sheets around. She shuffled and rearranged them.

Very soon she began to make discoveries. The meaningless lines on three of the drawings, placed one beneath another, suddenly became a picture. Nancy could see a tangle of trees, a large pool of water, and a winding path.

It was the picture, Nancy thought, of some remote tropical wilderness!

She searched for other clues. One of the trees seemed lopsided. It was fan-shaped, like a traveler's palm. But the palm had been neatly split in half!

Was that half-tree a clue? Nancy excitedly searched through the rest of the drawings. At last she found what she was looking for—the other half of the fan-shaped tree.

Edging the two sheets together to complete the tree, she made another discovery. The sheets placed together completed another picture.

And among the trees and branches was the distinct outline of three keys!

At another spot, where the sheets joined, Nancy found symbols representing the sun, a prostrate man, and a frog. The same figures on the note Terry found in the tent in Mexico!

"The person who wrote this diary somehow learned the directions to the Frog Treasure," Nancy thought wildly. "He didn't dare draw just one picture for fear somebody else would find out the secret!"

Feverishly she worked to decipher the whole picture message. Two other drawings, viewed separately, were nothing but irregular oval blobs. When the drawings were placed one beneath the other, however, the blobs suddenly appeared in pairs.

Footprints!

Six pair were leading—where? With painstaking care, she traced the footprints on another sheet of transparent paper. Then she laid them over the drawing of the tropical wilderness.

The result was just what she had suspected it might be. The circle was no longer empty. The footprints led to the rim of the large pool!

Then she placed the sheet over the second drawing, which revealed the keys and the symbols of frog, prostrate man, and sun.

This time the footprints led to the symbol of the frog!

She could hardly wait for her father to finish his work at the courthouse. She wanted to get home and talk to Terry Scott and show him her discovery.

When Mr. Drew came in, Nancy exclaimed, "Dad, I've pieced together the treasure map!" She added quickly, "Maybe Terry will recognize the location."

"Great work," the lawyer said. "You're really hot on the trail, but we must stay here until the day after tomorrow."

Friday the Drews caught an early plane for River Heights.

Mr. Drew went directly to his office. Upon reaching home, Nancy immediately telephoned Terry at his hotel.

"Mr. Scott hasn't been in for two days," the desk clerk informed her.

"Did he check out?" Nancy asked in amazement.

"Dad, I've pieced together the treasure map!"
Nancy exclaimed

"No, miss. He just hasn't been around."

Worried, Nancy asked Hannah if she had heard from Terry. When she learned no message had come, Nancy wondered if he had changed his mind about staying with the Wangells. She dialed the number, River Heights 7–4772. There was no answer.

Alarm for Terry's safety now made Nancy's heart beat faster. She telephoned George.

"I'm picking you up in five minutes," she told her startled friend. "I need your help on a search expedition."

Nancy quickly returned the obsidian key to her dressing-table drawer and locked the photographs in her desk, then hurried to her car. Within ten minutes she reached George Fayne's house. George was waiting at the curb.

"What's on your mind, partner?" she asked as they drove off.

"Worry," Nancy replied, and told about the disappearance of Terry Scott. "We're going to the Wangells'."

"Ugh!" George commented. "I see trouble ahead."

"We'll soon know," Nancy said.

She parked around the corner from the Wangells' house. Nancy rang the doorbell and they could hear creaking footsteps inside. But the footsteps hesitated and the person waited until Nancy rang again. Then the door flew open.

A red-faced woman with bleary eyes, her hair uncombed, stared out at them. Was this Mrs. Wangell? Nancy wondered.

"What do you want?" she asked suspiciously.

"We're looking for a friend," Nancy stated. "Terence Scott."

"Scott? Must be another house," the woman said and slammed the door. They heard a bolt slipping into place.

George grinned. "Seems as if we're not wanted."

"Wanted or not, I'm staying here until I do some investigating," Nancy decided. "Did you see those suitcases in the front hall?"

George nodded. "Maybe the Wangells are leaving town."

"If they are, it's for no good reason. George, Officer Riley is a block back at the intersection. Would you mind asking him to come here quickly?"

While George hurried away on her errand, Nancy circled the house. Dark shades were drawn and all the windows were closed with the exception of a small, second-floor one on the side. When she looked up at it, Nancy saw a curtain move, as if somebody were watching her.

Then suddenly her attention was directed to the top floor. Fluttering from an attic window was what looked like a man's white handkerchief!

Was it a signal of distress?

CHAPTER X

Nancy's Search

WHILE Nancy stood staring upward, she heard a car stop in front of the house and ran to see who was coming. It was a taxi. A man and a woman, each carrying a suitcase, hurriedly jumped into it. The Wangells were leaving!

"Wait! Stop!" cried Nancy, darting across the lawn.

Before she could reach them, the driver started off. Either he had not heard her, or he had been told not to pay heed to her call. The taxi gathered speed and disappeared around the corner.

Nancy dashed to her own car. She was determined not to let the Wangells get away.

When she turned the corner, the taxi was not in sight. Nancy drove on for several blocks, looking up and down the intersecting streets, but in vain.

"I'll try the railroad station," she said to herself and drove to it. Again no luck.

Her next stop was at the bus station. The Wangells were not there, and waiting passengers said no taxi had stopped at the place for over fifteen minutes.

"Maybe they went to the airport," Nancy thought. But a stop there gained her no information about the Wangells.

She decided that they must have engaged the taxi to take them out of town. The young detective hurried to the office of the Winfield Taxi Company. Perhaps someone on duty could communicate with the driver by radio. As Nancy dashed in, the girl at the desk looked up.

"One of your drivers had a call to 619 Fairview Avenue. Has he returned?" Nancy asked.

"No."

"Then please talk to him over your radio," said Nancy. "I must find out where his two passengers are going."

"And why should I do that?"

"Because it may save a man's life."

"Say, who do you think you are? An FBI agent?"

Nancy knew it was useless to waste any more time arguing with the girl. It would be better to get back to Fairview Avenue. George would be there with the police.

When she returned to the Wangell house, Nancy saw that George had arrived with Officer Riley, who said he had telephoned headquarters for help, since he could not leave his traffic post for long.

George burst out, "Hypers, Nancy, I've just about had heart failure. I thought you'd been kidnapped!"

"Have you tried to get into the house?" Nancy asked.

Riley nodded. "I rang the doorbell, but there was no response."

Nancy told them about seeing the couple leave the house, and that she was sure they were the Wangells.

"Did you notice the fluttering handkerchief?" she asked.

"Where?" Riley queried.

"I'll show you."

She led the way to the side of the house. The wisp of white cloth was no longer in sight!

"It was there. I saw it. Someone was waving it out of that attic window!" Nancy exclaimed, pointing excitedly. "I suspect someone is imprisoned in that house. I'm going to call and see if he answers."

Nancy cupped her hands to her mouth and made a yodeling sound. Then she called as loudly as she could:

"Terry! Terry Scott! It's Nancy. Can you hear me?"

The three held their breath, but not a whisper came from the shuttered house.

"Let me try," said George. She in turn called Terry, but there was no response.

Riley smiled tolerantly. "You sure you haven't been imagining things, Miss Drew?"

Nancy was indignant. "Of course not!" Once more she shouted, "Terry!"

There was no answer from the Wangell house. But next door a window was flung open and a stout woman leaned out.

"What is it?" she cried. "Is there a fire? Has something happened?"

At the same time an old man, with spectacles resting across his forehead, came bustling out.

"Say, why are you shouting?" he asked crossly.

Riley said, "These young ladies think someone they know is imprisoned in here. Have you seen the Wangells lately?"

The old man snorted. "Them? I don't pay them no mind. Don't like 'em. Phonies."

"What do you mean?" George asked.

"Just what I say. Not decent folks. Not neighborly. Not nice."

"But haven't you noticed anything?" Nancy persisted. "Your house is pretty close to the Wangells'. Are you sure you haven't heard any disturbance?"

The old man suddenly straightened. "Yesterday. I'd clean forgot," he said. "I thought it was my radio."

"Go on, mister," Riley prodded him.

"I was upstairs yesterday morning, taking my pills. And I heard somebody calling, 'Help, help!' Feeble and far away, you know. I thought, 'I've got interference. One of those stations cutting in and spoiling my music.' That's what I thought."

"Didn't you investigate?" Nancy asked.

"No, young lady. I just went downstairs and fiddled with my radio a bit and I didn't hear anything else."

"Oh, it was Terry! I know it was," cried Nancy. "Officer, we must go in the house."

The policeman still seemed doubtful. He was about to ask a question, when George gasped, "Look!" and pointed upward.

From the attic window the white handkerchief was once more flying its signal of distress. Riley, as well as the old man, stared wide-eyed.

"We won't wait any longer," Riley stated.

The stout woman who had yelled from the upstairs window now appeared on the scene. She was carrying an ax. Riley grasped the heavy tool and nodded his thanks.

He strode toward sloping double doors which led to the outside cellar steps. Testing the doors, he found they had been firmly barred on the underside.

"Stand away, everybody!" he ordered.

Riley took a mighty swing with the ax, and the heavy door shivered and splintered. Something on the other side fell away with a clatter. Riley pried one side of the door open and swung it wide.

"Stay outside, girls. There may be trouble," he commanded.

The officer descended the stone steps. Nancy and George could see the beam of his flashlight as he played it into the dark corners of the cellar. A moment later they heard the warning siren of an approaching police car.

Nancy turned to her friend. "George, I'm going inside with the officers."

"I'm with you," George declared.

They ran to the front of the house in time to see the police car stop at the curb. Four officers climbed out hastily. Two of them dashed to the rear of the house.

The girls met the other two at the front porch. One of these was Sergeant Malloy, who grinned at Nancy. "You still on the job?"

Officer Riley appeared at the front door and let them in, then left to go back to his post. Nancy hurried up the stairway, with George and two of the police following.

"Terry! Terry, are you all right?" Nancy called.

She expected an answer, but it did not come. The second floor was in semidarkness. Nancy felt along the wall for a light switch. At last her fingers touched a button. She pressed it, and light flooded a narrow hall.

"Terry!" she called again in alarm.

This time she heard something; not a voice,

but a muffled tapping sound. It was an answering signal and it came from above.

Nancy, George, and the policemen climbed to the third floor and began opening doors, but each one led to a closet or bedroom. Presently Nancy tried one which she found locked.

"This must be the attic door," she called excitedly. "And Terry Scott's up there. I know he is. Oh, hurry and open the door, officers. Please!"

Sergeant Malloy and Officer Trent braced their shoulders against it.

Several swift crashes of their bodies against the door broke the lock. With a splintering sound the door gave way.

CHAPTER XI

A Grim Story

NANCY was the first one up the narrow stairway to the attic. At her heels was Sergeant Malloy, his flashlight beaming the way ahead. The attic seemed to consist of a single storage room, low-roofed and windowless.

But among the shadows Nancy noticed a small door, the key still in the lock. While the police searched behind trunks and dust-covered chests, Nancy went toward the door and unlocked it.

As she did, there came a tap from the inside. Quickly she pulled the door open. A figure, bent over, stumbled toward her.

Terry Scott!

"Terry! Are you hurt?" Nancy gasped.

Though he shook his head, his face was deathly pale and his eyes looked dull and sunken. He tried to smile. One hand wandered feebly to his throat.

"You're ill!" Nancy cried.

The policemen carried him to a chair. Sergeant Malloy reached into a pocket and brought out a tiny glass vial. Nipping off the end with his thumbnail, he held the vial under Terry's nostrils and ordered him to take a deep breath.

Soon the color flooded back into Terry's face. His eyes brightened. He moved one hand to his throat.

"Lost my voice yelling," he whispered. "Thanks. You saved me from starving to death."

"Let's get him out of here," Sergeant Malloy ordered.

"I'll take him to my house," Nancy offered quickly as they assisted Terry downstairs.

"All right. Then I'll stick around here for a while," Malloy said. Turning to Terry, he added, "I'll get your full story later. Anything special you can tell us now?"

"Look for an old diary," the young scientist managed to say.

Nancy and George drove Terry to the Drew home. Hannah Gruen was concerned when she saw him. After learning that he had been without food for two days, she announced firmly:

"You leave him to me. I know what he needs."

Hannah insisted that Terry lie down on the living-room sofa. She put some chicken broth on the stove and made toast.

"How can I ever repay you, Nancy?" the young

professor murmured over and over after George had gone home.

"By resting and getting your voice back, so you can tell me what happened." Nancy smiled.

When Hannah returned with the food, Nancy announced that she had an errand downtown but would be back as soon as she could.

Nancy hurried out to her car and drove once more to the office of the Winfield Taxi Company. This time the blond girl at the desk was cooperative. She said to Nancy:

"Our driver Johnson just phoned in. He's at a farmhouse a couple of miles this side of Kirkland."

The driver had told her his two passengers from Fairview Avenue had forbidden him at gunpoint to turn on the car radio. They had ordered him to drive to Kirkland.

When they reached a lonely stretch of woodland, about three miles from Kirkland, Wangell had forced Johnson to stop, get out, and walk in the opposite direction.

"We're going to use your cab for a while, buddy," Wangell had said. "If you want it back, you'll find it parked in Kirkland."

Nancy asked the girl if the driver had notified the police. She did not think so.

"Johnson just called the office a minute ago."

Nancy leaned over the desk, picked up the telephone, and dialed the Wangells' number. Sergeant

Malloy answered. Nancy reported what she had just heard.

"I'll relay that to the police in Kirkland," he said, "and tell them to scour the town for the taxi, and the Wangells, too."

"Have you found out anything about them at the house?" Nancy asked.

"Not a thing. No sign of that diary the professor mentioned, either. By the way, the Wangells don't own this house. They only rent it furnished."

Nancy was disappointed. "Well, I'll appreciate your letting me know if anything turns up."

She was glad to learn, when she returned home, that Mrs. Gruen's care had worked wonders with Terry. He looked like himself again.

Nancy pulled up a hassock and sat down beside him. "Don't strain your voice," she cautioned, "but please tell me in a few words what happened at the Wangells'."

"They must have suspected what I was doing and planned to imprison me until they could get away," he replied.

"How did they manage to get you to the attic?"

"As you know, there were several pages missing from the diary. Mrs. Wangell said that they might be in the attic with some other old papers. So I went with her to look."

"And Mr. Wangell sneaked up after you and locked you in?" Nancy asked.

Terry nodded grimly. "Yes, but before he locked the door we had a scuffle. Wangell gave me a knockout punch. I don't know how long I was unconscious. When I started coming to, my brain seemed very foggy."

"Drugged," Nancy guessed.

"I think so," Terry answered. "Wangell was standing over me, laughing. It was an awful feeling. He kept asking me questions about the cipher stone. I knew I mustn't give him any information."

Terry went on to say that he had found out a few things about the Wangells, however, before his capture.

"They hate each other, for one thing. I'm sure of that. Listening to them talk was like waiting for an explosion. There was constant tension between the two, even when they weren't quarreling. Mrs. Wangell seemed to be afraid of her husband."

"Why?"

"I couldn't figure out why, but every time she started to find fault with him, he would stop her with a stunt that would send her into a panic. I'll show you."

Terry walked over to the Drews' piano. Clenching his right hand into a fist, he ran his knuckles along the black keys, hitting them in a loud, quick glissando.

"How strange!" Nancy murmured.

"After Mr. Wangell did that, he'd laugh uproariously," Terry explained. "It had the strangest effect on Mrs. Wangell. She'd clap her hands to her ears and scream 'No, Earl, no!' as if she were in pain."

"Go on," Nancy urged.

"Here's something a bit more definite," Terry continued. "I think Mrs. Wangell and Mrs. Porterly are sisters."

Nancy was amazed. She praised Terry's detective work and asked, "How did you find out?"

"I listened, the way you suggested. Mr. and Mrs. Wangell talked a lot about Miami and a couple down there named Will and Irene. I deduced that Will was short for Wilfred Porterly."

"And his wife?"

"That was easy. Once when the Wangells were arguing, I heard her say, 'You should have listened to Irene and me. We Webster girls at least have common sense.' "

Terry said he had remembered Mrs. Prescott saying that Mrs. Wangell was Lillian Webster.

"Oh, Terry, this is wonderful!" Nancy exclaimed.

"Glad you think so," he replied, grinning.

"I wonder if the Wangells are on their way now to join the Porterlys in Miami," Nancy mused.

She told Terry about the Wangells' treatment of the taxi driver, and also that the police had searched the house but had failed to turn up the diary or any other clues.

Suddenly Terry remembered Nancy's trip to Baltimore. He asked what she had learned there.

"That was just a trick to get us out of town," Nancy answered. "I came back a little too soon for the Wangells. Or did I?" She smiled ruefully. "They got away."

"But you saved me," Terry whispered. His voice was giving out again. "You saw my handker—" The rest was lost.

Nancy insisted he rest again, promising a big surprise at dinnertime that evening. Terry Scott slept for three hours, awakening just as Mr. Drew walked in. The lawyer was deeply concerned when he learned what had happened.

"I had no idea your enemies would go to such lengths," he said to Terry. "It's amazing what evil men will resort to in trying to acquire a treasure."

This reminded Nancy of her promise to Terry. She brought out the photographs of the diary pages and the tracings she had made from them. Terry was intrigued by the footprints leading to the traveler's palm; the symbols of the frog, the prostrate man, and the sun; and the three black keys.

"Amazing!" he murmured.

After studying the complete drawing which

Nancy had made, Terry shook his head. "I've never seen a spot that looks like this one," he said. "Too bad it has no directions or points of the compass on it. If I could only locate the cipher stone—"

Nancy brought out her copy of the slip of paper she had found in the shrubbery with its mysterious notation "5 x 7 and one." Terry could make no more out of it than he had the first time.

Mrs. Gruen announced dinner and they all went to the table. As soon as the meal was over, Mr. Drew drove Terry to his hotel. He promised to retire at once.

At eight o'clock the next morning Terry called Nancy on the telephone. For a moment she feared something had gone wrong, but he soon reassured her.

"I did a lot of thinking last night," he said. "I feel I should return to Mexico. The Mexican police haven't sent me any report. Maybe they have given up the search for Dr. Pitt. I must find out."

Terry said he had a nine-o'clock plane reservation, and was leaving for the airport at once.

"I hate to say good-by this way," he added. "You've been such a good sport, Nancy. But I hope next time I see you, I'll have good news."

Terry said that if she did not hear from him soon, she would know that he was deep in a Mexican jungle looking for his scientist friend.

"Don't you want to take the half-key with you?" Nancy asked.

"No. I might lose it. If I need the key, I'll send for it. Anyway, I feel that I'm not going to solve this whole mystery in Mexico. There will be many things you'll have to clear up if you will. I'm depending on you."

"Terry, are you sure you'll be safe?"

"Now don't worry," he said, laughing. "Well, I must say good-by now."

After she had put down the telephone, Nancy sat lost in thought. No matter how she looked at it, she had a strong hunch Terry's sudden decision to start for the jungle was unwise. What could he do alone against ruthless enemies?

CHAPTER XII

A Hard Decision

AFTER Mr. Drew had been told of Terry's decision, and had left for his office, Nancy reviewed in her mind the swift-moving events of the past twenty-four hours. What was there she could do to help solve the mystery, now that Terry was returning to his explorations in Mexico?

"I can still try to find out where the Wangells went," she decided. "That may lead to the Porterlys and then to Juarez Tino, and—"

Her thoughts were interrupted by the ringing of the telephone. Sergeant Malloy reported failure in locating the Wangells.

"The Kirkland police thoroughly searched the town. No clues to where those folks went. You got anything else to suggest?"

"Florida."

"What?"

"My guess is," Nancy replied, "that the Wangells will join the Porterlys in Florida."

Malloy seemed to be intrigued with the idea that the two wives might be sisters. He said the police would communicate with Florida authorities to try to find the couples.

"We have a report on Wilfred Porterly," the officer went on. "His driver's license is okay. But according to the records, he hasn't owned a car for years, so the car registration was forged and the license plates stolen."

"Did the Miami police find him at his home?" Nancy asked.

"No, but they'll keep an eye out for him. Remember that Tropical Sun Fruit Company that Porterly talked about? There's no such business in Florida."

"What is his business?"

"A lot of pretty fancy rackets. At one time, for instance, he was connected with some art dealers."

"The Wangells," thought Nancy. After she had thanked the officer for calling and hung up, she said to herself, "And now the 'fancy racket' is cashing in on an old treasure."

When Bess and George dropped in a few minutes later, Nancy was improvising idly on the piano in the living room.

"George told me all about yesterday," Bess said excitedly. "She says Terry left town. Oh dear, I wish I'd been home for the excitement, but I suppose I'd have been scared green."

Nancy smiled, but made no comment.

"You wouldn't be feeling lonesome for Terry, would you?" George asked slyly. "Or is it the plainclothesmen you miss? I notice they've left."

"They're on duty only at night now," Nancy answered. "But I'm not lonesome. I'm trying to puzzle something out. Bess, do you know what five times seven and one are?"

"Why, thirty-six."

"Yes. And I've just been counting, Bess. There are exactly thirty-six black keys on the piano."

She told the girls about Mr. Wangell's method of frightening his wife. "Like this." Nancy illustrated by running her knuckles over the black keys as Terry had done the day before.

"Nancy, are you trying to say there's some connection between that slip of paper you found in the shrubbery and Wangell's trick of scaring his wife?" George asked.

"I don't know. But that stunt at the piano must have reminded Mrs. Wangell of something very unpleasant. Maybe some sort of a threat."

"Nancy, you make me positively shudder!" Bess declared.

"How would you two like to take a trip to Florida?" Nancy asked her friends suddenly.

"Love to," George declared. "But my bank account would never stand the strain."

"Neither would mine after that trip to New York." Bess sighed.

George changed the subject. "How about a little tennis to take your mind off the mystery?"

"Not now," Nancy replied. "I have some heavy scheming to do!"

"Well, we're off to the courts," Bess said.

"Don't think *too* hard!" George teased as the girls waved good-by.

But Nancy was soon deep in thought about the mystery. She was more eager than ever to carry on a search in Florida. After lunch she broached the subject to her father.

"Dad, do you suppose you could manage a Florida vacation next week?"

"I'm afraid not," he replied. "I must be in court Wednesday."

"Then how about my taking that field trip with Dr. Anderson? It sounds interesting. If he lets me join his students, will you give me money for the trip?"

The lawyer's eyes twinkled. "If I furnish the capital, seems to me I deserve a statement of some kind. Are you really so fascinated by Indian culture—or do you want to keep your eye on Dr. Anderson?" he teased.

"All right, Dad. I'll own up. You'd never let me go to Florida alone."

"And?"

"You see, it's not just Dr. Anderson who is

heading for Florida. My guess is that Wilfred Porterly is there this minute. And the Wangells are on their way."

"I see," Mr. Drew said. "But what made you think of getting to Florida by trying to join Dr. Anderson's group?"

Nancy said there were several reasons. She believed it was not just his duties as a teacher that were taking Dr. Anderson to Florida. It might well have to do with the mystery of the black keys and the Frog Treasure.

"Maybe we can work together," she said. "Anyway, if I locate the Wangells, I may need a man's help."

"Right you are," the lawyer agreed. "Well, if you go with the class, I'll give you the money. But I'm wondering if Dr. Anderson will permit it. You're not a student of his, my dear."

Nancy smiled confidently. "No. But several who are going on the trip are specials. They come from various places." She gave her father a hug. "Thanks a million," she said. "I'll phone for an appointment to talk it over."

When Nancy faced the professor in his office the following Monday morning, she did not feel so confident, however. Dr. Anderson was not very cordial.

"I suppose you know, Miss Drew, that you are a bit late. The students who have registered for the trip have already completed their preparatory work."

"I know it's highly irregular, Dr. Anderson. But I've done some reading about American Indians, ancient and modern. And I was hoping you'd accept me as a sort of special student."

The professor narrowed his eyes. "Isn't your interest in this field trip a bit sudden?"

Nancy could not help smiling. "I'll be honest with you, Dr. Anderson. It's not only interest in your subject that prompted my visit. I want to do some research of my own in Florida. And I need you as a sort of—bodyguard."

Perhaps it was Nancy's smile—or her show of honesty—that brought about a change in the professor's manner. He softened. There was a suggestion of compromise in his voice when he spoke again.

"As you say, it is highly irregular. But I'll tell you what I'll do."

"Yes?" Nancy asked hopefully.

"I'm giving my students here a quiz on the work we've covered so far. If you can pass that quiz, you may accompany us to Florida."

Nancy's pulse quickened. "I'll try it," she said. "Thank you."

CHAPTER XIII

Smoke Screen

"WHEN is the quiz?" Nancy asked Dr. Anderson.

"This afternoon at three," the professor replied.

Nancy looked at her watch. It was ten-thirty. She had a few hours to study!

Eager to use her time to advantage, Nancy hurried to the college library. There the librarian pointed out the books used for Dr. Anderson's course in American Indian Culture.

"And this should help you," the woman said, giving Nancy a typewritten sheet. "It's an outline of the work covered each month."

The syllabus stated that the subjects assigned for the past month were *The Aztecs of Mexico* and *Early Indian Tribes in Florida.*

Fortunately, Nancy had brought a notebook and her fountain pen. She read all the chapters on Florida Indians, and made notes on the facts which seemed most important about the ancient Aztecs.

She hardly took time for lunch, studying her notes while she ate a sandwich in the cafeteria. After lunch she returned to the library and did more reading until it was time to go to class.

As the students flocked in to take their seats, Dr. Anderson arose from behind his desk.

"Please remember that none of you will be given special consideration," he said, looking straight at Nancy. "If you know the subject, you will pass. If you do not know the answers, you will fail."

He gave out the quiz sheets and the blue notebooks in which the students were to write their answers. Nancy's hours in the library, she discovered, had been well spent. She was able to answer all the questions except the last: *Who were the Zapotecs? Where and when did they live?*

She did not remember having read anything about the Zapotecs. Terry Scott had never mentioned them.

She had to leave the question blank!

At the end of the period, Professor Anderson asked the students to put their quiz books on his desk. When Nancy left hers, she hoped he would speak to her. But his only response to her smile was a stern nod.

"He'll be a hard marker," Nancy thought woefully.

"How did you make out?" a friendly girl asked.

Nancy sighed. "I couldn't answer the question about the Zapotecs."

"Anderson's a mean old crow for asking that one. It wasn't in the lectures—he just said we could look it up."

"Pretty shrewd," Nancy commented, then introduced herself.

The girl said that she was Frances Oakes, and she introduced her two friends as Marilyn Maury and Grace James.

"Are you coming to Florida with us?" Grace asked hopefully.

Nancy said that she planned to go if she passed the test.

"That's the big 'if' for all of us," Marilyn said with a sigh.

"I'll never stand the strain of waiting until to-morrow!" Fran groaned. "That's when the quiz grades will be posted."

"What time?" Nancy asked.

"Dr. Anderson said they'd be posted by five o'clock," Fran answered. "I'll call you as soon as I know them myself."

That night was a restless one for Nancy. Next morning, she decided to look up the answer to the question she had missed. From the encyclopedia she learned that the Zapotecs were an important tribe of Mexican Indians. They had resisted invasions by the Aztecs and their culture had been one of the highest in that country.

After reading the article, Nancy's hopes sank. "That does it," she thought. Her ignorance would seem inexcusable to Dr. Anderson. She would flunk the quiz.

"And Dad will never let me go to Florida alone." She sighed.

At lunch Carson Drew noticed that Nancy was not eating with her usual appetite. "Is that quiz on your mind?" he asked kindly.

Nancy admitted that it was. Then she changed the subject and tried to act cheerful. But after her father had left for his office, she looked at her watch anxiously. How could she spend those four long hours, waiting for Fran to call?

Nancy had just settled down to a new novel when, shortly after one-thirty, the River Heights fire siren blasted. Mrs. Gruen came hurrying from the kitchen.

"It's our district," the housekeeper announced. "That fire must be right in this neighborhood."

She and Nancy rushed out to the front porch. Black smoke was pouring from the Hackley house, two doors up the street.

Nancy and Hannah raced across the lawns, reaching the scene just before the fire engines. From somewhere in the rear of the house, Nancy heard a woman screaming. Leaving Mrs. Gruen, she ran to the back door. Mrs. Hackley came staggering out, carrying her year-old baby. The woman and her infant were crying hysterically.

"Let me help you," Nancy offered and did her best to calm them.

Meanwhile, the firemen had gone inside the house. Presently one of them ran out of the cellar carrying a bucket full of black, smoldering rags.

The fireman approached Mrs. Hackley. "Here's your trouble," he said. "Know anything about this?"

Mrs. Hackley stared. "N-no. Where did you find that?"

"These rags were stuffed into a duct from your furnace. They've got oil on them and some sort of chemical. That's what made the terrible smoke in your house."

"Mercy!" cried Mrs. Hackley. "Whoever would do a crazy thing like that?"

Nancy shuddered. The Drews' front door had been left open. The firebug might have gone into their house!

Not seeing Hannah, Nancy hurried home alone. Quickly she went to the kitchen and opened the cellar door. There was no sign of smoke. She was breathing a sigh of relief when she heard a stifled cough.

Nancy's heart pounded. Was the man who had started the fire at the Hackleys' starting a fire here?

Then another thought came to her. Had he set

"Let me help you," Nancy offered

the Hackley fire to lure her and Hannah away so he would have time to look for something—and steal it?

Nancy thought with regret of the plainclothes-man who had been on guard during the day. If only he had not been dismissed!

She tiptoed through the kitchen, and cautious-ly crept across the lower hall and up the carpeted stairway. As she reached the upper hall, Nancy saw a man emerge from her bedroom.

The intruder turned, saw her, and stiffened. Juarez Tino! He was clenching something black in his hand.

Terry Scott's half-key!

CHAPTER XIV

Danger and Diplomacy

JUAREZ TINO gasped in astonishment. He stood irresolute, then wheeled around and started for the back stairs.

"Oh, no, you don't!" Nancy cried. With a lightning lunge she was after him, reaching for his clenched right hand.

"Give me that key!" she demanded.

"I will not!" Juarez muttered.

Nancy was desperate now. She tore at his right hand with both of her own and managed, for a moment, to wrest the key from the man's grasp.

But not for long. With an angry oath, Juarez wrenched his arms free and pushed her violently through the bedroom doorway. Prying her fingers loose, he once more took possession of the key, dropping it into his breast pocket.

"Help! Help!" Nancy screamed, hoping Mrs. Gruen was near the house.

"That won't do you any good." Juarez leered

triumphantly, and forced Nancy to her knees. "I'll teach you," he sneered.

His knee against her back, he sent her sprawling face downward. Then he seized both her hands and pinned them behind her. With his necktie, he quickly tied her wrists together.

Nancy twisted and thrashed away from him. Though she was powerless to escape, the struggle delayed him a few seconds. She tried to scream again, but Juarez clamped a hand over her mouth.

"When I get through with you, you won't be able to talk," the swarthy man threatened.

He whipped a handkerchief from his breast pocket to gag her. Nancy saw the half-key fly through the air. Then he gagged her, and she did not see the key land. Juarez, apparently, did not know he had lost it.

Next, he tore a blanket from her bed and stretched it on the floor. He rolled her over and over until it encased her from toes to shoulders. Then he tied it with a sheet.

At that moment the front door slammed, and Hannah Gruen called, "Nancy, are you home?"

Muttering to himself, Juarez pushed Nancy out of sight under the bed.

"You should have stayed at the fire a while longer, Detective Drew," he sneered.

Creaking footsteps told Nancy he was sneaking down the back stairs. If only she could scream Hannah's name! She could barely moan.

Nancy desperately tried to roll out from under the bed. She heaved against the night table and shook the lamp. The noise brought Mrs. Gruen to her side immediately.

"Nancy!"

Hands trembling, she removed the gag from the girl's mouth. As Hannah untied the sheet, Nancy explained what had happened.

"Juarez Tino started that fire and tied you up?" Hannah Gruen cried. "If I ever get my hands on that—that—!"

She flew to the window. Not seeing him, she rushed to the telephone. As Mrs. Gruen dialed police headquarters, she stormed:

"They shouldn't have let that daytime plain-clothesman go. Leaving you here at the mercy of that maniac!"

Nancy got to her feet stiffly, rubbing her arms to bring back the circulation. She stood deep in thought, wondering about the key. It was not in sight. Had Juarez discovered his loss and retrieved the key?

Hopeful that he had not taken the precious relic with him, she examined every inch of carpet. The key was not in sight.

Hannah called, "Nancy, I have Sergeant Malloy on the phone. He wants to talk to you."

The officer asked a number of questions about Juarez Tino. He said he would put several of his men on the trail immediately.

"We'll comb this town," he declared. "I'll be up to see you later."

After Nancy had hung up, Mrs. Gruen joined in the search for the missing obsidian key. When neither of them could find it in Nancy's room, they were forced to conclude that Juarez must have taken it with him.

Nancy was blaming herself for not having chosen a safer hiding place, when she heard a car in the driveway. Glancing from the window, she saw Sergeant Malloy step out. Hannah admitted the policeman and brought him upstairs.

"You found Juarez?" she asked hopefully.

"Not yet, but the men are out looking. I stopped in to get a full report on what happened, and to tell you we heard from Savannah, Georgia."

"About the Wangells?"

"No, the Porterlys. The police there say a couple who gypped a gas-station attendant, and rode off just before the police got our message, were probably the Porterlys. The Savannah police are trying to track them down."

"I thought they were already in Florida," Nancy said. "I wonder when the Wangells expect to meet them."

The officer said he wished he knew. Malloy made an examination of the premises. He was just leaving when George and Bess came in. When Nancy walked outside with him to conclude her conversation, Mrs. Gruen told the two cousins the story.

"Hypers!" said George when Nancy returned. "Talk about a cat having nine lives! This must be your forty-ninth!"

"That awful man!" Bess wailed. "He might have killed you!"

George gave her friend a searching glance. "You don't seem very happy," she remarked. "Aren't you glad to be safe?"

"I'm afraid Juarez took the key with him. Terry will never forgive me!"

George and Bess made Nancy tell everything that had happened, moment by moment. They ended re-enacting the drama together, with Nancy's bedroom key substituting for the black half-key.

George suddenly had an inspiration. "Which blanket did Juarez use?"

"The dark navy one from my bed."

George spread the blanket on the floor. Caught in the fleecy wool was the black half-key! It was hardly noticeable against the navy color.

"George! You found it!" cried Nancy, delirious with joy.

In the midst of the excitement, the telephone rang. Hannah answered, then called up the stairway, "It's for you, Nancy. The girl says her name's Frances Oakes."

Nancy sobered at once. On the way to the telephone in her father's study she tried to calm herself.

This was a decisive moment. She was about to learn whether she had passed Dr. Anderson's quiz. Upon this call would depend her chance of a trip to Florida to continue her quest for the black keys and the Frog Treasure!

"Hello, Fran," Nancy said into the telephone, her heart thumping. "What's the news?"

"Nancy, you made it! I don't see how you did it without going to class. But you passed!"

Nancy had to giggle, she felt so relieved. "I was lucky, I guess. How did you girls make out?"

"We passed, and we're thrilled you're going to Florida with us."

Nancy asked when the trip would start.

"Dr. Anderson has chartered a morning plane for day after tomorrow. It leaves from the airport near the Institute," Fran replied. "Why not spend the night at my dorm?"

"Wonderful!" Nancy exclaimed. "I'll be there. Any special clothes I should bring?"

"A few cotton dresses, slacks or dungarees, and high-laced boots for trips in swampy terrain. The going will be rough in some places, Dr. Anderson says. Snakes and things."

"Mm! What else?"

"Bring a bathing suit—naturally. Say, do you like to water ski?"

"Love to."

"My cousin Jack Walker who lives in Miami has a motorboat," Fran said. "When we're not working, maybe we can go out with him."

Nancy promised to meet Fran at her dormitory for dinner the next evening. Then she said good-by, and hurried to tell the good news to Bess, George, and Hannah.

"I don't envy you one bit!" exclaimed Bess. "I'm afraid of snakes."

"When I was about ten years old," said George reminiscently, "my family took me to Key West." Suddenly she snapped her fingers. "Maybe the treasure is buried on one of the Florida Keys!"

"What treasure?" Bess asked.

"The Frog Treasure. The ancient secret which Terry thinks is hidden in a silver frog."

"I thought it was in Mexico," Bess said. "You mean Juarez Tino found out where it's buried?"

"Or buried it there himself after he brought it from Mexico," George replied. "Remember how Wangell scared his wife, striking those black keys on the piano? Maybe it was a sort of pun."

"You mean," Nancy spoke up, "that Wangell knew the story from Juarez and might have been reminding Mrs. Wangell of something that happened on a *Black Key* in Florida?"

"Exactly."

"The way the reminder bothered her, the happening must have been pretty bad," Bess declared. "Burying a treasure isn't so awful."

"That's right," Nancy said, frowning. "There must have been something more to it than just that. But anyway, if Juarez Tino had the treasure, why would he still want the half-key?"

"I didn't think of that," said George.

Nancy decided to look at a map of the area to which she was going. Perhaps an answer to the problem would present itself. She went to the bookcase for an atlas. She quickly flipped the pages to a detailed map of the Florida Keys.

As the cousins looked over her shoulder, Nancy ran her finger along the many Florida islands, scanning them quickly for their names.

She sighed. "No Black Key yet."

"Here it says 'Ten Thousand Islands,'" Bess remarked. "I wonder if all of them have names."

Once more Nancy ran her finger along the fine print of the map. No Black Key listed. But probably many of the small islands had names known only locally, she concluded. As soon as she reached Florida, she would find out if there were an island called Black Key.

It was possible that such an island might be uninhabited and unexplored. A perfect spot for hiding a captive—like Dr. Joshua Pitt!

Long after Bess and George had left, Nancy continued to brood over this possibility. Alternately she was excited about the prospect of finding the elderly professor hidden there, and afraid he might have been starved or tortured by Juarez Tino and his friends.

A voice from the second floor brought her back to reality. "If you don't come and see about your clothes, Nancy, you won't be ready to go."

"Coming, Hannah."

Nancy went upstairs and picked out a few summer dresses, skirts, slacks, and sweaters. Then as Hannah started the packing, Nancy went downtown to buy heavy, high-laced boots.

Upon her return, Hannah told her that Ned Nickerson had telephoned. Hearing of Nancy's plan to join Dr. Anderson's expedition at Clifton Institute, he had decided to come down and drive her there.

"He's expecting to take you to lunch and spend part of the afternoon with you," the housekeeper reported. "That means you'll have to be ready early."

Next morning, after kissing her father good-by and promising to write often and not take dangerous risks in her sleuthing, she and Hannah went to Nancy's bedroom to finish the packing. As the housekeeper opened the young detective's handkerchief drawer, she found Terry Scott's half-key.

"While you're away, it seems to me you ought to put this in a safer place," she advised.

"You're right," Nancy admitted. "From now

on, I'm going to know where it is every minute."

She fastened the half-key securely to a narrow but strong, flesh-colored ribbon. Then she tied the ribbon and slipped it over her head, hiding the key inside her blouse.

"I should have thought of this before Juarez came here," she told the housekeeper.

Nancy was ready to leave. Bess and George arrived and wished her a wonderful trip. Ned came and they drove off.

The hours sped by pleasantly. Before Nancy realized it, the time had come for Ned to leave her at Frances Oakes's dormitory.

"Good-by and good luck," he said. "Wish I were going to Florida."

After a leisurely evening and breakfast with Fran and her friends, Nancy taxied with them to the airport. Dr. Anderson was there and most of the students who were taking the trip.

When they were taking seats, Nancy selected the one next to Dr Anderson. She said, "Do you mind?" and pretended not to notice when the professor gave her a cold, unfriendly stare.

The engines roared and the plane sped down the runway and lifted gently into the sky.

Nancy waited for the professor's face to unfreeze in a smile. But he stared straight ahead.

"I'll have to use diplomacy if I'm ever to win his friendship," she thought.

Aloud she said, "I looked up the answer to the

question I missed on the quiz. About the Zapotecs." The professor merely nodded.

Then Nancy mentioned the Indian tribes in
Florida. She spoke guardedly of a diary which described their legends. It had been written, she
said, partially in an Indian tongue.

"Might have been Timucuan," growled Dr.
Anderson. "At the time of the conquest, Timucuan was the language known all over Florida."

After he said that, his face flushed and his eyes
got fiery.

"Look here, Miss Drew, why don't you admit
you've been working for Terry Scott—that you
still work for him? Are you meeting him in
Florida?"

"No," Nancy said quietly. "Terry has gone to
Mexico."

Dr. Anderson exclaimed, "Mexico! What has
he found out? Why has he gone back there?"

When Nancy did not immediately reply, he
burst out petulantly, "I suppose he took that half-
key with him. He has no right to it!"

CHAPTER XV

The Helpful Fisherman

NANCY winced. Terry had no right to the obsidian key? Who had a right to it if Professor Scott did not?

If Dr. Anderson only knew that the key was not two feet from him, he might feel even more disgruntled and suspicious than he was!

"Terry Scott has no more right to it than Dr. Graham and I have," Dr. Anderson continued in an angry tone.

Nancy breathed easier. Smiling, she said, "Perhaps not. But someone has to keep it."

"Well," the professor said testily, "Terry Scott is acting mighty secretive about the whole thing. Why didn't he inform me that he was going to Mexico?"

Nancy tried to keep her voice calm and unruffled. "As you know, Terry is on leave from his classes at Keystone this year. While you and Dr. Graham are busy with your teaching, he naturally feels that he ought to be trying to solve the ancient mystery."

"He'll make certain that he appropriates the honor and the glory, too," Dr. Anderson complained bitterly.

"I'm sure that's not his intention, Professor," Nancy said, assuring him that Terry's main concern was the disappearance of Joshua Pitt. Both she and Terry were fearful the doctor was being held a prisoner.

Dr. Anderson did not agree. He still had a feeling that the elderly professor was hunting for the treasure by himself.

"Anyway," Nancy went on, "I'm sure that as soon as Terry learns anything definite, he'll tell both you and Dr. Graham."

"That old fuss-budget!" the professor scoffed.

Nancy laughed. "You know what I think, Dr. Anderson? You're all jealous of one another. Talk about Terry being secretive! I'll bet right now you have a secret you're not telling either Terry or Dr. Graham."

A slow flush came to Dr. Anderson's face, and Nancy pressed her advantage.

"For instance, this trip to Florida. You have chosen that spot for the field trip because you think that something—or someone—is hidden there. Haven't you?"

The professor was taken by surprise. He turned to peer at her, a startled look in his eyes.

"For a girl your age, you seem to know a lot of answers." He sighed. "I may as well admit the truth. I suspect the treasure may be buried in Florida, and Dr. Pitt and Juarez know this."

"Why?"

Dr. Anderson told her that during Juarez Tino's call on him at Clifton, the man had accidentally dropped a hint. He had mentioned the fact that the ancient Indians of Mexico and Florida had a great deal in common in their state of civilization.

"I'm sure he didn't figure that out himself," Dr. Anderson said. "He got it from Pitt. Right away I suspected he'd been with Pitt in Florida and was double-crossing him."

"Did you accuse him of that?" Nancy asked excitedly.

The professor nodded. "Juarez swore he hadn't been near Florida. But I knew he was lying."

"Wouldn't he tell you anything about Dr. Pitt?"

"He was so furious at me for guessing it, that he raised his price. That was when I threw him out of my office."

"I can't blame you for that," said Nancy. "And it fits right in with a theory of mine." She told about Terry and the Wangells and the trick on the black piano keys. "But I'm positive Dr. Pitt and Juarez are enemies, not friends."

She also told him about the warning message at the Drew house, and of her recent encounter with Juarez, when he had bound and gagged her, and shoved her under a bed.

"He'd probably treat a man even worse," she added.

Dr. Anderson's eyes widened. "I don't mind saying I admire your spunk," he remarked. "And I like the way you think things through. What would you say to our joining forces in Florida? Terry can't object to that, while he's in Mexico."

Nancy agreed willingly, and the professor told her that the study group would have their headquarters at the Southern Skies Guest House in Miami. From there, they would take trips to museums and Indian villages to study the culture of present-day Seminoles.

"Of course I'll do a bit of detective work on the side," he told Nancy, and added slyly, "I suppose you'd like permission to do the same."

Nancy was thrilled. Everything was turning out so well!

"And now that I've let you in on my secret, young lady," Dr. Anderson said, "how about telling me yours? What is your special project in Miami?"

"I'm afraid it's not very definite," Nancy admitted ruefully.

She told him about her discovery that the Wangells and Wilfred Porterly were heading for Florida. She also showed him the diary drawings which might possibly have a connection with the treasure.

"Of course it's just a hunch," Nancy said. "But if there is a Black Key down there, I think it may be the hiding place we're seeking. I'd like to hunt for it."

The professor stared in horror. "Explore the Keys—by yourself?"

Nancy laughed. "Not exactly. I was hoping you'd give Fran Oakes and me a separate assignment. We could study Indians too—the ancient Indians on the Keys."

Anderson shook his head. "That would still be unwise. Two girls alone!"

"Fran has a cousin, Jack Walker, who lives in Miami," Nancy explained eagerly. "He has a boat, and knows the bay. He could act as guide and protector."

Dr. Anderson smiled. "That's different," he said. "I'll talk to Miss Oakes's cousin when we get to Miami, and if he seems the proper sort, I think we can arrange things."

After that, the professor yawned a few times and began to doze. Even Nancy, excited as she was, at last went to sleep. When she awakened, the other students were excitedly scanning the view far below them. Nancy left her place by the professor and walked back to take the vacant seat beside Fran Oakes.

"Pines and lakes and palm trees," Fran said. "We must be over Florida."

Nancy told her new friend that Dr. Anderson might allow them to go exploring together on a field trip of their own.

"Do you think Jack Walker would take us in his motorboat?" she asked.

"He'd love to!" Fran declared.

After a hearty lunch on the plane, the travelers landed in Miami. The Southern Skies Guest House, where Nancy and five other girls were to stay, proved to be a very attractive place. Its palm-studded yard sloped to the edge of a pleasant inland waterway.

"Jack can bring his motorboat right to our door, Nancy," Fran Oakes cried happily.

Mrs. Young, the guest-house owner, showed Nancy and her friends to two double rooms, then told them to make themselves comfortable. The girls thanked her, unpacked, then went for a swim.

That evening the student group assembled in the dining room of a hotel up the street. Professor Anderson outlined some local points of interest, then gave the students their assignments for the following days.

Nancy was awakened the next morning by Fran, who told her that Jack Walker was coming to the hotel at eight o'clock. They took quick showers and dressed.

Jack proved to be a good-looking man in his early thirties, serious-minded and athletic. Dr. Anderson seemed to take a liking to him.

"Miss Oakes and Miss Drew want to arrange their own field trip," he said. "If you can give them some time, I'll grant permission."

"I'll take the job—my boat's in A-1 shape." Jack grinned.

They skimmed over the blue water for two hours. Nancy tried to map out in her mind the complicated waterways of the area, but admitted defeat. At last they returned to the dock.

"I wish we could do our research on water skis." Fran sighed.

Jack wanted to know what the research was. "It had better be interesting," he teased.

"Nancy is treasure hunting," Fran explained. "She's looking for an island called Black Key. Know where it is?"

"Never heard of it. But I know the right man to tell her. His name is Two Line Parker."

"What a funny name!" Fran giggled.

Jack took them to see the bearded old fisherman, who lived in a tiny white cottage on the waterfront. His eyes twinkling, he told them how he had received his curious nickname.

"I kin manage two lines at once," he boasted, "just as easy as most folks handle one. Tell you 'bout the time I got me two big fish, one on the left side o' the boat, one on the right side. They was tuggin' so hard, I thought they'd pull me clean apart."

"Did you bring both fish in?" Nancy asked.

"Sure did," said Two Line. "I just tied those two lines together and let the fish fight it out. When they got tired, I pulled 'em in easy."

The old fisherman laughed uproariously and winked at Jack. Then he asked what he could do for them.

"This young lady," said Jack, indicating Nancy, "is looking for treasure on the Florida Keys. Have you any ideas, Two Line?"

The old man became thoughtful. "I don't rightly know where to lay my hands on any at the present. But a heap o' treasure has been buried time and agin on the Keys."

"What kind of treasure?" Fran asked.

"Smugglers' stuff. The Keys used to be a great place for smugglers. And then there was the pirates. They'd make raids on the cargo ships that passed this way."

"Didn't our Navy try to capture the pirates?"

Two Line Parker chuckled. "Sure, but for a long time they couldn't catch 'em. Those pirates was smart. They used shallow boats so they could sneak into the narrow channels of the Keys.

They'd hole up there, after they'd made a raid. The big ships couldn't follow 'em. They'd have grounded if they had."

Jack asked who finally got rid of the pirates.

"Commodore Parker, back in 1824. He built a fleet o' barges and some light-draft schooners. Went after them pirates and cleaned 'em out in no time."

"And that was the last of the pirates?" Fran asked.

Two Line Parker smiled wryly. "I wouldn't say that. Ever hear of the Florida reef wreckers?"

The girls shook their heads.

"I used to know a couple of 'em myself. Wrecking captains, they was called. Here 'em talk, you'd think they was kind and honest. They'd keep boats ready. When there was a wreck, they'd sail out and rescue the folks on the doomed ship."

"What was wrong with that?" Jack wanted to know.

Two Line Parker snorted. "It wasn't just the folks they wanted to save, Jack. It was the cargo. Why, there was plenty of wreckers in the old days, what would lure ships onto the reefs at night with false signals. Wreck 'em on purpose, for the cargo."

"How horrible!" Nancy cried indignantly.

"So you see, all sorts of things have happened on the Keys. Treasure hid and treasure stolen, I reckon. Any special Key you were thinkin' of, young lady?"

"Do you know of a Black Key?"

Two Line Parker scratched his head. "Never heard tell of that one. I could name you hundreds. But Black Key—"

Then suddenly the old fisherman remembered something. "I tell you what, though. There's that Key where the *Black Falcon* was sunk, back in the eighties, in a hurricane. I never heard a name for it, but Black Key'd be a good name on account of the *Black Falcon*."

Nancy was very excited now. This might be the place for which she was searching!

"But if I were you, young lady, I'd—" Two Line paused, shaking his head.

"You'd what?" Nancy prompted him.

"I'd stay away from there—I'd stay as far away as I could get!"

CHAPTER XVI

A Burned Letter

INSTEAD of being frightened by the fisherman's warning, Nancy found her curiosity aroused about the island. She asked Two Line Parker why he had advised her to stay away from it.

"Stories they tell," he answered. "The place is haunted, some folks think. Take that ship, the *Black Falcon*, the night she sank. I've heard Indians talk about it. They say a fire rose up out of her even when she was under water. And after that it rained frogs."

"Frogs?" echoed Jack Walker, and Nancy wondered if the old man's mind were not wandering.

"You don't believe me," Two Line said. "Well, it ain't just me that says so. It's writ down, sure enough, in a book."

"Who wrote it down?" Nancy asked suspiciously.

Two Line nodded his head wisely. "Old sailor

down here. Dead now. Lived on the Keys for years, just writin' everything down. Stories the Indians told mostly. He knew their language like his own, and Spanish, too."

The old man's final sentence caught Nancy's attention.

"Who was he? What was his name?" she queried.

"Evans, they called him. Never knew his first name. He went everywheres listenin' to stories and writin' 'em down."

"Had he been a sea captain?" Nancy asked excitedly.

"I don't rightly know. Never talked about himself. When I knowed him, he'd lived around here for years."

"And he kept a diary?"

"Maybe that's what it was. He made drawin's, too. He'd fool hours away, adrawin' and ascriblin'. But he'd never show that book of his to nobody."

The old man babbled on about Indians, pirates, and shipwrecks, but Nancy kept thinking about Evans, and the "book" he kept. It could very well be the diary Mrs. Wangell had in her possession!

"What happened to the diary?" she asked.

Two Line had no idea.

"Would you please show us, on a map, where the *Black Falcon* was sunk?" Nancy requested.

Jack Walker had a map of Florida in his pocket. He unfolded it and handed the flattened sheet to the fisherman.

Two Line Parker squinted at the shoreline, and pushed a calloused forefinger over a scattering of small Keys.

"About here. There's a Key nearby, I seem to remember, that's called Storm Island."

Nancy marked the spot on the map with her pencil, and decided to ask Dr. Anderson to accompany her there the following day.

But the professor had other plans for Saturday. He told Nancy that he had chartered a bus for a visit to a Seminole Indian reservation. Fran and Nancy, he insisted, were to join the other students on the trip.

Though she was reluctant to spend the time this way, especially since the next day was Sunday and Dr. Anderson had ordered a day of rest, Nancy found the trip a fascinating one.

Sunday evening, while eating supper with her friends in a tearoom, Nancy decided to make a start on her detective work. She took a notebook from her purse and found the address Wilfred Porterly had given to Sergeant Malloy at the River Heights airport.

Fran Oakes groaned. "Watch out, girls. Nancy has a plan. I can see it hatching."

Nancy laughed. "How would you three like to go on a manhunt with me?"

"With bloodhounds?" Grace James grinned.

"No. Just with our own wits."

"Whom are we going to hunt?" Marilyn asked.

"A man named Wilfred Porterly and his wife Irene," Nancy replied. "Not respectable, I warn you."

"Let's go!" said Fran. "It's a better game than just sitting around at Mrs. Young's."

In high spirits, the girls left the tearoom and hailed a bus which carried them north on Biscayne Boulevard. A few minutes later they got off and after a short walk reached a neat, Spanish-style bungalow.

The four girls walked up the steps and Nancy rang the doorbell. They heard footsteps inside, and the door was opened by a woman with a mop in her hand. She looked surprised to see her four callers.

"Good evening. Are you Mrs. Wilfred Porterly?" Nancy asked, eying the mop.

The woman smiled. "Mercy, no. I guess you're looking for the former tenant."

Nancy showed her disappointment. "Did the Porterlys move out recently?"

"Two weeks ago yesterday."

The woman set down her mop. "You'll have to excuse me. I'm busy cleaning. I have to clean day and night, they left the place so dirty. I guess they moved out in a hurry."

She took a slip from her apron pocket. "I

found this on a nail in the kitchen. I guess it's their forwarding address."

Nancy read the notation: "Porterly, c/o General Delivery, Florida City."

"I suppose you don't know the Porterlys personally?" she asked.

The woman threw up her hands and made a face. Then she looked embarrassed. "I hope you're not friends?"

"Not exactly," said Nancy. "We came on business."

She and the other girls said good night and walked back toward the boulevard.

"Florida City," said Grace. "That's too far away for tonight."

"Any other criminals we can hunt? In Miami that is," Fran teased.

"Perhaps," said Nancy. "If I can find his address."

While the other girls waited, Nancy stopped at a drugstore telephone booth and looked for the names Juarez Tino and Conway King in the Miami directory. They were not listed. When she called Information, the operator said that neither person had a telephone.

"The missing persons," Nancy told her friends, "will have to stay missing until tomorrow. Let's go back to Mrs. Young's and get some sleep."

Next day Dr. Anderson promised Nancy that he would accompany her and Fran on their trip to find Black Key. But he could not start, he said, until after lunch.

"Would it be all right if Fran and I spent the morning in Florida City?" Nancy asked. "It's only a few miles from here and we could rent a car."

The professor gave permission, and shortly before ten she and Fran were speeding through the picturesque area south of Miami.

Parking their hired car along the palm-lined main street of Florida City, Nancy and Fran went in search of the post office. But no help was to be gained from that quarter.

"Sorry," said the clerk. "We can't give you any information."

"I might have guessed," Nancy told her friend. "We'll just have to do our detective work the hard way."

Someone, somewhere, Nancy hoped, would have seen or heard of the Porterlys. She asked a policeman, but he shook his head.

She tried a drugstore, a gas station, and a sandwich shop, but none of the personnel had heard of the Porterlys. After that, she visited a market and a candy-and-stationery store, again to no avail.

"I don't see how you can be so persistent," Fran said. "I'd have given up ages ago."

Nancy chuckled. "That's the fun of being a detective. You look and look and keep on looking. And suddenly, when you least expect it, you find a clue."

They next inquired at a small souvenir shop selling Florida shells and curios of various kinds. Nancy repeated her usual question.

"I'm trying to locate a man and his wife who, I understand, are staying in Florida City. Their last name is Porterly."

As had happened so many times, the proprietor shook his head. But a young boy who was sweeping the shop spoke up politely.

"I think I can help you, miss. I delivered a package to a Mrs. Porterly just last week. She was staying at the Sunland Tourist Home."

He gave directions for reaching the house. The two girls hurried to their car and drove away quickly.

"Now we're getting somewhere," Nancy said triumphantly.

But her triumph was short-lived. They found the tourist home boarded up and deserted. Nailed over the Sunland sign was a neat card which read: *Closed Temporarily. Will reopen December 15.*

"What do we do now? Go back to Miami?" Fran asked gloomily.

"Not yet," Nancy replied. "Let's look around."

She went to the porch and peered into the mailbox. It was empty. Then she and Fran walked toward the back yard.

In the middle of the driveway stood a wire incinerator. Evidently it had been in use recently, for it smelled faintly of smoke. Upon investigation Nancy found that a pile of letters had been burned. Some of the envelopes had not been entirely consumed by the flames.

"It won't hurt to look," Nancy told Fran. "Here—hold my shoulder bag, please."

She turned the incinerator on end and upset the contents in the driveway. Then she singled out the letters which had partially escaped the fire. Seating herself on the back steps, she began to examine them.

Most of the scraps proved valueless. But one envelope excited her interest. It read:

"Mr. W. Port—" The rest of the address was seared.

Nancy looked inside the crumbling folds of paper. Only a scrap of the letter had survived. But its contents startled her.

> Drew girl and
> the trail. Cover you
> Will meet you at B
> the fifteenth.

Nancy's heart thumped wildly. *Drew girl!* Were the Porterlys and their friends plotting some new evil against her?

"The fifteenth is day after tomorrow!" Nancy cried. "Oh, Fran, if only more of that letter hadn't burned, we'd know where Porterly and someone else—probably Juarez Tino—are going to meet. And why!"

Nancy put the scraps of paper in her purse, and the girls returned home.

"Nancy, it all sounds as if you were in dreadful danger," Fran said worriedly as they went to lunch.

"I admit I must be very careful. But if a lot of us stick together, no harm can come to me," the young detective assured her. Fran perked up. By two o'clock they were out on the bay in Jack's boat with Dr. Anderson.

On the way to the spot where so many years before the *Black Falcon* had sunk, Jack pointed out various sights to the girls.

"Over there is what's called a sea garden," he was saying. "It's very pretty. Grasses, coral, ferns, starfish, and conch shells."

The roar of a speedboat, passing a few yards at their left, almost drowned out his words. Nancy looked up curiously—and her back stiffened.

In that brief moment, as the boat rushed by she had glimpsed the dark, sinister face of someone she knew. Nancy caught Dr. Anderson's arm.

"That man in the boat!" she cried, pointing excitedly. "He's Juarez Tino!"

CHAPTER XVII

The Elusive Island

As THE speedboat passed, Juarez Tino turned to look back. Had he recognized Nancy?

"Follow that boat!" Dr. Anderson ordered.

Jack opened the throttle and his boat leaped ahead, its prow out of the water.

"Glad to speed. But why?" he asked. "Is that man ahead someone you know?"

"We think so," Nancy answered. "Keep him in sight if you can."

An idea suddenly came to her. The note in the incinerator had said "Will meet you at B—" Was Juarez heading for Black Key?

They raced after his speedboat, following its zigzag course. Then Juarez disappeared behind a palm-fringed islet. When the others rounded it, he was not in sight. They cruised in the vicinity for a while, searching for him, but he had vanished.

"We'd better not waste any more time," Nancy

said. "I think Juarez went straight on to the Black Key. Let's look on the map for Storm Island."

After studying it, Jack headed the motorboat west, but could not find the Key which Two Line had vaguely pointed out on the chart. After an hour he changed his course. "You'd have to be a wizard to know this place thoroughly. Shorelines keep changing. New Keys building up."

"How does that happen?" Fran asked.

"Tides, storms, shifting sands. And the busy mangrove tree. That's the great land builder in these parts."

He pointed to the junglelike growth edging the Key they were passing. "Mangrove roots grow fast and spread faster. They catch drifting plant life and debris. And so the shoreline keeps building up."

About twenty minutes later, Nancy asked, "Are we nearing the place where the *Black Falcon* sank?"

Jack shrugged. "That Key we just passed is Storm Island. And out there near one of those Keys, according to Two Line Parker, lies the *Black Falcon*." He pointed toward a vista of islets.

"But don't ask me which one," Jack added with a grin. "You'll have to figure that out yourself."

He wound in and out among the islands. But since Two Line had told them nothing specific about the surrounding Keys, it seemed hopeless to identify Black Key.

They watched for Juarez, and listened for the drone of his speedboat. But all they heard were the cries of cranes and the lonely wail of limpkins.

"It's lonesome out here," Fran said. "We must be miles from civilization."

Dr. Anderson looked at his watch. "I think we'd better start back."

Nancy felt frustrated as Jack headed his boat toward Miami. The hunt had certainly been disappointing.

"But," she told herself, "I'll come back. The fifteenth isn't until Wednesday."

Nancy told Dr. Anderson about the charred letter she had found in Florida City that morning.

"According to that, Porterly and his friends are meeting on the fifteenth at some place beginning with a B. It may be Black Key," she declared.

"Sounds reasonable," the professor agreed. "Perhaps we should come back tomorrow and continue our search. We may be able to pick up Juarez's trail."

Nancy was delighted that he had expressed her own desires. "But let's get an early start," she said. "In the morning."

Dr. Anderson frowned. "You forget I have other students. I'm taking my class to a museum in the morning. We'll have to wait until afternoon."

"How about Fran and me going out in the morning with Jack?" Nancy proposed.

The professor shook his head. "Now that I know Juarez is around, the answer is No. Two men in your party is the absolute minimum."

When they reached the dock of the Southern Skies Guest House, a familiar figure came to meet her.

"Terry Scott!" Nancy was dumfounded.

The young man grinned. "Like a dutiful daughter, you wired your dad. So when I talked to him on the phone, he told me where I might find you."

Nancy introduced him to Fran and Jack. "And of course you and Dr. Anderson—" she added.

The older man gave Terry a long, cautious stare. Then, smiling, he held out his hand.

"I guess we may as well be partners," he said. "I've been using the services of your young detective on my own."

Terry laughed boyishly. "With the three of us working together, we can't lose."

"What have you been doing, Terry?" Nancy asked as they walked to the house. "We haven't heard a word from you."

"I'll tell you at dinner," he promised. "How about you and Fran and Dr. Anderson eating at my hotel?"

Half an hour later they gathered in the big

dining room. Terry picked up the menu card and smiled.

"Ummm. Pompano steak, corn bread, and papaya!" He sighed appreciatively.

After a waiter had taken their orders, Nancy said, "Now tell your news."

"First of all," Terry began, "a good lead came from the Mexican police. They told me about an old woman—an aunt of Juarez—who lives a few miles from the site of our excavations. They have a signed statement from her."

She admitted that Juarez had stolen the cipher tablet and Dr. Pitt had trailed him. She knew this, because Juarez had stopped at her place for food to take on a journey and had told her the story.

"Did she know where Juarez was going?" Nancy asked eagerly.

"No. She had no idea where either Pitt or Juarez might be found."

Nancy smiled impishly. "Dr. Anderson and I can do better than that. *We* know where Juarez is."

Terry looked at her in amazement. "In Florida?"

Nancy told about the pursuit of Juarez and their fruitless search for him in Jack's motorboat.

"I'd like to go out myself and hunt for him," Terry declared. "Do you suppose, Fran, that your cousin would take us all out tomorrow morning?"

Nancy threw Dr. Anderson a demure look. "I'm sure Jack will go, but the professor is conducting class tomorrow in a museum."

Early the next morning Jack Walker moored his boat at the guest-house dock. Terry and Nancy were waiting, and Fran hurried to join them at the last minute, pencil and notebook in hand.

"The prof is making me write a report," she said. "Otherwise, I can't go with you."

Jack started the motor and the boat sped off on its mission.

"What's the subject?" Terry asked. "Maybe we can help you."

"The Florida Keys—Their Character and Their History."

Terry smiled. "All right. Let's start with their character. The Keys are small coral islands stretching some two hundred miles beyond the mainland. At one time they were probably part of the land link to Yucatan."

Fran looked at Terry thankfully. "Gracious, I didn't know that!"

Nancy reminded the girl of Two Line's stories about pirates and wreckers, and Fran wrote busily in her notebook.

At last the searchers reached the group of Keys they had visited the afternoon before and started cruising around. Finally Jack let the motor idle.

"Hopeless," he said.

"It's a maze, all right," Terry agreed. "But let's not give up."

Nancy pointed toward a small craft near one of the islets. "Could that be Juarez?"

Jack headed his boat in that direction, and they soon overtook the other boat. It proved to be a small fishing cruiser, and Juarez was not aboard. Its only occupant was a sun-tanned fisherman, obviously intent on the day's catch.

Nancy addressed him with a smile. "Good morning. We're doing a little exploring. Would you please tell us how to find the Black Key?"

"Black Key? Never heard of it, miss."

"Perhaps you know where the *Black Falcon* was sunk many years ago?" Nancy asked hopefully.

The man in the cruiser grinned. "It's fishing I like, not history," he said. "It's enough if I know the Keys by their shape, so to speak, and how they're arranged. It helps me remember where the catch is good."

"Well, thank you, anyway."

Jack Walker was about to pull away from the other boat, when Nancy remembered something—the slip of paper she had found in the shrubbery at home, with the notation "5 x 7 and one."

"I have one more question, if you don't mind," she called to the fisherman. "You spoke of knowing how the Keys are arranged. Is there any place where they're in groups of five and seven—and then one Key lying alone?"

The man frowned, and thought about this. "Five and seven. Well, I'll be switched! That's the way they are, though I never figured it out before."

He pointed with his rod.

"There's five of them over that way, spreading south and eastward. They're in a kind of half-moon. And yonder there are seven more of those Keys, sort of chainlike. They run north."

"And the single island?" Nancy asked.

"I'm not sure about that one," the man answered. "There might be a single one in there somewhere. I don't remember."

Nancy told the fisherman he had been very helpful, and Jack turned his boat in the direction the man had pointed out. Soon they reached the five half-moon Keys and the chain of seven Keys.

"Now let's look for that odd island," Terry said. He was becoming intrigued, too, by the possibility of solving the mystery of Black Key.

Jack cruised slowly around the inside of the half-moon. There, overshadowed by the larger Keys and at an equal distance between the two groups, was a tiny islet.

Nancy was so excited she could hardly speak. "This must be Black Key!" she whispered.

Viewed from the boat, the spot looked like a small jungle of mangroves. But as they approached, its extent proved to be greater than they had supposed. Searching its shadowy rim, they at last found an opening in the dense growth.

Jack guided his motorboat into the narrow inlet. Sheltered by the trees, they were completely out of sight of passing boatmen.

"A wonderful hideaway for pirates like Juarez!" Terry commented.

Nancy spotted a path that wound off among the trees and suggested that Jack stop. "Let's get out here," she said in a low voice, "and do some exploring."

The group disembarked and cautiously moved inland. For a short distance the path wound and twisted among the mangroves. Then it suddenly ended at an open, sandy knoll.

Nancy and her companions stood still and gazed around them. In a moment Nancy pointed through a tangle of bushes across the clearing.

"Look!" she whispered.

Almost concealed by the surrounding trees was a low gray hut. As they dashed across the open space toward it, the searchers heard a plane overhead. It was flying low.

"Hide!" Terry commanded. "We don't want to be seen."

CHAPTER XVIII

The Hidden Hut

EVERYONE ducked beneath the concealing shelter of mangroves, but Nancy was afraid her group already had been spotted.

"If Juarez was in that plane, there may be trouble for us," she declared.

The seaplane circled the island several times, then droned off.

"Looks bad," Terry said. "We'd better hurry and see what's on the Key before the plane returns."

Once more he and Nancy crept toward the hut, with Fran and Jack following. Fran was frightened and nervous.

"Is this what detective work is like?" she asked. "Why, you take your life in your hands!"

Terry said nothing, but he agreed. He had not forgotten the episode at the Wangells'!

The hut ahead was about the size of a two-room

bungalow and built of heavy weather-worn timbers. "Driftwood from wrecked ships," Nancy mused. There was one small window in the front and a low door.

Terry knocked. No answer. He put his hand on the latch and pushed. The door opened. The four walked inside.

They stood in a small room, unfurnished except for two canvas deck chairs. In one corner lay a pile of newspapers and magazines—most of them in Spanish—and a carton of canned goods.

"Somebody's been here recently," Fran Oakes whispered. She pointed to the window sill.

A half-eaten candy bar was being consumed by black ants. Beside it stood a bottle of soda, half empty.

Suddenly they heard, from somewhere in the hut, a shuffling sound. Terry motioned toward a heavy door with an old-fashioned, primitive bolt. It apparently led to an inner room, and someone was in there!

"You two girls stand back," Terry whispered.

As he started to open the door, a hoarse voice cried out:

"Go away! I won't tell you!"

Nevertheless, Terry swung the door open. Jack followed him inside. Then came Terry's astonished voice:

"*Dr. Pitt!*"

Nancy and Fran dashed forward. Seated on a

cot was a haggard, elderly man, his eyes sunken but with a determined, fiery light in them.

"Thank goodness you found me," he said, deep emotion in his voice. "But I don't know how you did it."

Eagerly Terry introduced the old man to his friends. Joshua Pitt gave them a sad, wry smile.

"Welcome to my prison cell on Black Key!"

He pointed to a small hole in the roof, too small for escape, and the meager furnishings in the room—the cot and two packing boxes which served as table and chair. One of them held several cans of food.

Dr. Pitt explained that Juarez and two other men had held him captive, trying to make him tell them where the Frog Treasure was hidden.

"Were the other men named Porterly and Wangell?" Nancy asked.

"Yes. Porterly was here twice, Wangell only once. But I wouldn't tell them a thing," the elderly professor said proudly, "no matter what they did."

Terry asked eagerly, "Dr Pitt, did you learn the ancient secret we were trying to find out?"

Dr. Pitt's eyes flashed defiantly. "I know. But I won't tell anyone—not even you," he announced. "No one shall ever force the secret from me."

"But why not?" Nancy asked, astonished.

"Because it would mean the destruction of mankind," the archaeologist replied.

The two men helped the elderly professor to one of the deck chairs in the outer room.

"At least tell us," Terry begged, "how you came to be captured."

Joshua Pitt said that the night following the afternoon he and Terry had found the cipher tablet, he had translated the message on the Mystery Stone. He had learned that the secret was one of evil. The professor refused to say more about it.

Terry asked, "While you were making your translation, did you drop a paper with notes on it?" He described the symbols of the frog, sun, and prostrate man.

"Yes. Those symbols are the clue to the secret." Joshua Pitt frowned. "Because of that I decided to keep the three black keys. But in removing them from their ring, I broke one of them."

Nancy said that she had the half-key with her. Fingering the ribbon at her throat, she explained that Terry had entrusted it to her.

"How did Juarez steal the cipher tablet?" Terry asked.

"After I made the translation," Dr. Pitt said, "I hid the stone tablet under a blanket. Juarez must have been watching me. As I dozed off, I heard a noise. It was Juarez making his escape. I knew at once what had happened and I started after him."

"Why didn't you yell?" Terry asked.

Dr. Pitt admitted that was where he had made his mistake. Thinking he could handle the situation alone, he had not awakened the others.

"But Juarez turned the tables," he said wryly. "I followed him to some old woman's house—she was a relative of Juarez. He and a Mexican pal ambushed me, packed me into a plane, and brought me here."

"And the cipher tablet, too?" Terry wanted to know.

"Yes. It is buried on Black Key," came the startling announcement.

"Do you know the spot?" Nancy inquired excitedly.

"I have no idea," Dr. Pitt replied.

Nancy asked when he expected Juarez back.

"Tomorrow."

The fifteenth! But he might come sooner, Nancy decided. If the man in the plane were a spy, Juarez would come as soon as he got the word!

Dr. Pitt's eyes smoldered. "Juarez said tomorrow would be my last chance. He was bringing friends here to make me tell my secret by torturing me some devilish way."

Fran Oakes shivered, and Terry, frowning, looked at his watch. He turned to Jack Walker.

"See here, Jack. We can't leave the cipher tablet on the island. How about you and Fran taking the boat and getting the police? Bring

them here as soon as you can. In the meantime,
Nancy and I will hunt for the tablet."

Jack nodded. He and Fran hurried from the
hut.

Joshua Pitt turned to Terry. "Now that I've
told my story, how about yours? I'm curious to
learn how you knew I was here."

"The credit belongs to Nancy." Terry smiled.
"She did a smart bit of detective work."

At Dr. Pitt's insistence, Nancy told the story
herself. At the end she asked, "Why did Juarez
bring you to Black Key?"

"He knows this area well. Used to come here
years ago, looking for pirate gold. I fancy Juarez
is a bit of a pirate himself."

"But why Black Key?"

"A friend of his owned an old diary. That
must be the one you were translating, Terry.
Don't you remember about the *Black Falcon*?
There was something in the story about frogs, and
Juarez got the idea it might mean the Frog Treasure and it was hidden here. But they won't find
it on Black Key because it's buried elsewhere."

Terry looked puzzled. "Wait a minute," he
said slowly. "The Wangell diary made no mention of the *Black Falcon* nor any frogs in connection with it."

"Juarez showed me the pages. He must have
torn them out of the diary before you saw it."

"That's the answer!" Terry exclaimed. "When

Mrs. Wangell showed me the diary, several pages were missing."

Pitt went on with his story. "Juarez has the two good obsidian keys, and the broken half. Heaven help the world if he ever finds the other half, and becomes master of the secret!"

Nancy longed to know the nature of the secret, but the stern look on the scientist's face warned her not to ask. Instead, she decided to go outside and look around for clues to the buried cipher stone.

As she reached the doorway, Nancy heard a step outside. Before she had time to slam the door, a woman rushed in. Her strong arms encircled Nancy's neck in a strangle hold and forced her back into the hut.

"Now I've caught you!" she yelled at Nancy. "We saw you and your boy friend from the plane."

Terry reached for her arm, but he was too late. Three men sprang at him. While two pinioned his arms to his sides and bound them with rope, the third stood by dumfounded, as if he had seen a ghost.

"Will! Juarez!" he cried. "It's Professor Scott!"

"Yeah," Porterly said in disgust. "You thought you'd fixed him for good, didn't you? Get to work!"

Nancy was bound hand and foot, then Earl Wangell tied up Joshua Pitt.

Strong arms encircled Nancy's neck in a strangle hold

The woman pushed Nancy roughly against the wall. "I'm Mrs. Juarez Tino," she snarled. "Does that mean anything to you?"

Nancy did not answer.

"Think you're clever, don't you?" the woman cried. Mrs. Tino started to drag the girl to her feet, then changed her mind.

"I'll search you first," she said in her brassy voice. "You still have the key we want."

Seeing the ribbon around Nancy's neck, she tore off the obsidian relic with a savage wrench.

"Now we have everything!" Juarez exclaimed triumphantly. "The fortune is ours!"

CHAPTER XIX

Threats

PORTERLY, Wangell, and the Juarez couple dragged their prisoners from the hut, and through some dense underbrush to a clearing.

The captives were ordered to sit side by side. Juarez began to dig in the earth with a shovel.

Nancy's heart sank, but she was determined not to show it. There was one gleam of hope. Only two of her group had been spotted from the plane. These people did not know that Fran and Jack had gone for the police!

"It won't do you any good to dig up the tablet," Dr. Pitt said. "You can't translate the message."

Juarez gave him a sneering look. "You'll tell us. We'll use Nancy Drew as a new means of persuasion," he said meaningfully.

"The police know all about you," Terry warned him. "For instance, they know it was Porterly who knocked me out at the hotel, stole my papers, and then broke into the Drew home."

"And they know, too," Nancy added, "that Juarez calls himself Conway King. That's how we found out you caused our accident on the road to Emerson!"

"Count me in on that." Wangell smirked.

Nancy wished she could look at her watch. It seemed a long time since Jack and Fran had left to go for the police.

"They ought to come any minute," Nancy thought. "We must play for time." Aloud she said, "You tried to break into our home in River Heights one night, Juarez."

"That old woman of yours with her homemade burglar alarms!" Juarez growled. "If it hadn't been for her, I'd have got the key that night."

"But we have it now!" Mrs. Tino cried, showing it to her husband.

Juarez's face broke into a smile. He signaled Wangell to take over the digging. Then he came and stood in front of Nancy.

"Even if you hadn't walked into this trap, I had plans for taking care of you."

"I know," Nancy said quietly. "You sent a note to Wilfred Porterly. But he didn't do a thorough job when he burned that letter in Florida City."

Just then Wangell's shovel made a ringing sound, and a moment later he lifted a large stone slab from its hiding place. It was decorated with grotesque carving and mysterious symbols.

Nancy's heart was pounding. Now that these thieves had the tablet, they might leave the island and take their prisoners along. And the police had not arrived! She must delay these people if she could.

"Well, I guess we're ready for our trip," Juarez said. "First my boat, then the plane."

Even seconds counted now! Nancy asked calmly who had mailed the fake letter from Baltimore, using an innocent old man's name.

"A friend." Juarez smiled in satisfaction. "But nobody could ever prove it."

Juarez made a sign to his companions, picked up the stone tablet, and proceeded down a narrow path. The Tinos, Wangell, and Porterly followed with their three captives.

The path led to the opposite side of the island from the one where Nancy's party had landed. A cabin cruiser was anchored a short distance out.

The prisoners' ankle bonds were removed, and they were forced to splash through the water and go aboard. They were crowded into the cabin, then the ropes were replaced and tightened securely. Wangell started the motor.

"You know where to head," Juarez said. "Porterly's place."

As the cruiser pulled away from Black Key, he

chose a seat on a bench between Nancy and Dr. Pitt.

"Now, Joshua Pitt," Juarez sneered, "tell us what you know. Where's the ancient treasure?"

Nancy cried out, "Don't tell him! Don't tell—"

Juarez raised his hand as if to strike Nancy.

"Stop!" Dr. Pitt cried. "I'll tell you. Go to Mexico. You'll find the treasure in Mexico." He named a site near the center of a little-known jungle region.

Juarez got up and stood over Dr. Pitt. "You're going with us to Mexico. Tomorrow morning we start looking for the treasure! If your directions are wrong, Professor—*you'll be to blame for what we'll do to Terry Scott and Nancy Drew!*"

By this time the boat had reached another Key. A red-faced, nervous woman, whom Nancy recognized as Mrs. Wangell, met them. She cried out in astonishment upon seeing Terry.

"It can't be! It can't be!" she wailed.

"Shut up!" Mrs. Tino commanded. "Help me take the girl."

Nancy was half dragged, half carried through a grove to a yellow cement bungalow. Terry was brought in by Juarez and Wangell, while Porterly remained on the boat to guard Dr. Pitt.

An evil smile contorted Juarez's face as he turned to leave. "My little wife, you know what to do with these prisoners."

He and Wangell left, closing the door behind

them. A few minutes later Nancy and Terry heard the cruiser churning away from the dock. They were lined against the wall, while the women surveyed them.

"See here," Terry said. "Be reasonable. Those ropes are cutting Miss Drew's wrists."

Mrs. Tino's face set grimly. "We'd better separate these two." Motioning to Mrs. Wangell, she said, "Take the girl into the bedroom."

Mrs. Wangell did as she was directed. The door swung shut behind them.

"Maybe I can get her to talk," thought Nancy. "She's not cruel like the others." Smiling disarmingly, she said, "I know you don't want to do things like this, Mrs. Wangell."

The woman looked at the floor. "No, I don't. But Earl makes me. Oh, I don't know what to do. He and Juarez shouldn't have kept Dr. Pitt a prisoner. It might have killed him."

"It's a serious offense," Nancy said. "By the way, Mrs. Wangell, where did you get that interesting old diary?"

The woman became silent, as if listening for eavesdroppers from the other room. Then she whispered, "Juarez stole it from a man named Evans. After he tore out some pages, he gave it to me."

"And asked you to have Terry Scott figure out from it where a certain fortune was?"

Mrs. Wangell admitted this, saying he also

wanted to keep Terry busy, so he would not hunt for Joshua Pitt.

Nancy heard an airplane. It came closer, flying so low over the bungalow that the walls vibrated. Mrs. Wangell ran to the window.

"There they go!" she exclaimed. "Oh, I hope Dr. Pitt's wrong that something dreadful is going to happen when they find the fortune! Earl is so foolish!"

Nancy pressed her advantage. "Mrs. Wangell, why are you so afraid of your husband?"

The woman hung her head. "I once stole something. But only Earl and Juarez know about it."

"I see," Nancy said. "Nevertheless, I advise you to turn state's evidence when the police round you all up. You'll get off easier."

Mrs. Wangell looked frightened. "Earl didn't mean to be bad after he got caught once."

"About the paintings?"

"Yes. It's just that he hooked up with Juarez. Juarez knew Earl had me in his power. He used to play the black keys on the piano to remind me of Pitt being a prisoner. Then Earl took it up. It was awful—"

The door burst open.

"You'll pay for this, Lillian, you tattletale!" cried Mrs. Tino. "I'm going to fix you and the Drew girl after I've taken care of Terry Scott!"

CHAPTER XX

The Three Keys

WHEN Mrs. Tino rushed to attack Mrs. Wangell, she screamed and dashed into a closet. Quickly Juarez's wife sprang to the lock and turned the key.

Almost simultaneously, Nancy saw Terry in the doorway. He had finally succeeded in loosening his bonds.

As Mrs. Tino flew at him in a rage, she tripped over a chair and fell to the floor, stunned. Terry rushed to Nancy's side and untied the rope on her hands. With her hands free, she wrenched at the knots around her ankles. Then while Terry tied the woman's ankles together, Nancy bound her wrists.

Nancy looked at him gratefully. "Thanks for rescuing me. I'll never forget it," she said. "But we mustn't delay here."

"You're right," Terry agreed.

He noticed a fishing rod in a corner. "Nancy, give me a white handkerchief. I'll rig up a distress signal."

It took only a few seconds for him to attach. Then he and Nancy ran from the house.

"I see a boat out there," Terry called. "It looks like a police launch."

He waved the fishing pole wildly. The boat came toward them.

There were six figures on deck—Fran, Jack, and four policemen!

"That white flag handkerchief did it," one of the officers said when the boat docked. "We couldn't find you."

"Oh, we've been frantic!" Fran cried. "We went to Black Key and there wasn't a sign of you. We've been searching everywhere."

Nancy knew there was not a moment to lose. Hurriedly she and Terry explained what had happened and said they must get back to Miami at once.

"We'll take care of those women at the house," the sergeant in charge said. He radioed a report to headquarters, then told one of the men to take the young people to the Key where Jack had left his boat.

The fastest possible speed was made. When Nancy and her friends transferred to Jack's craft, Terry urged him to use all the power it had, saying:

"Nancy, Dr. Anderson, and I have a date in Mexico. We must reach the treasure spot before Juarez gets there with Joshua Pitt."

Dr. Anderson met them at the dock in Miami, anxiety on his face at their long absence. While Terry telephoned to charter a plane, Nancy told the professor what had happened. His eyes were wide with amazement.

"Do you think we can get there in time?" he asked.

"We'd better," Nancy said grimly. "We have several hours. The others won't begin work before morning."

Dr. Anderson dashed to a telephone and got in touch with a retired friend. After a few minutes' conversation he returned to the others.

"Miss Oakes, please tell my students that Dr. Lewis White will take over the work while I'm gone. And," he added, "will you get in touch with Dr. Graham long-distance at Jonsonburg and tell him the developments here? Ask him to come to Miami if possible. We'll be in touch with him here."

Fran promised, then fearfully said good-by to Nancy. "Oh, do you have to go? Something dreadful might happen to you!"

Nancy assured her friend she would be in safe hands. Then she hurried to the waiting plane with Terry and Dr. Anderson.

About dusk the three alighted at a small airfield in the interior of Mexico. Three uniformed police officers hurried to meet them, and spoke in Spanish to Terry.

"They'll have a car waiting for us at the crack of dawn," Terry told the others. "We'll go by a short cut the men know to the spot where Juarez is heading."

Nancy and the professors were escorted to a hacienda by the police. After a late supper they retired immediately in order to be fresh for the task of the following day.

They were awake before daybreak, and by the time the red sun shone over the jungle, the party was on its way.

Nancy, Terry, and Dr. Anderson climbed into a mud-spattered station wagon, while the police took the car ahead. They rode into the jungle until the path dwindled to a one-man trail.

Terry consulted the police, then translated, "The officers say we can ambush Juarez at Diablo Point."

Single file, Nancy and the five men hurried along the trail. At a fork in the trail, the police halted. They told Terry that Juarez and his friends would have to pass there, to reach the site mentioned by Joshua Pitt. It was suggested they all hide in the undergrowth, and nab Juarez and his accomplices as they came by.

For a long time nothing happened. The jungle air was hot and oppressive. Trailing vines tickled

Nancy's neck where she lay, and gnats and mosquitoes attacked her ankles.

She began to worry. Perhaps they were too late. What if Juarez and his cronies had already reached the treasure spot! Perhaps, at that very moment, they were torturing Joshua Pitt—

Then she heard the distant tramp of feet, the sound of a voice. Peering through the dense growth, she saw men approaching. Joshua Pitt was in the lead, head bent, feet dragging. He seemed to be in the last stages of exhaustion.

Behind him came Juarez and his pals. Wangell had several tools in his hands. Porterly held a shovel and a large burlap bag.

As they came near, Joshua Pitt said in a cracked, weary voice, "I don't know the exact location. Anyway, the secret will destroy mankind, I tell you!"

Wangell sneered, "Then that power will be ours. And we'll have the treasure, too!"

"Professor, you're lying about not knowing!" Juarez snarled. "Do you want Nancy Drew to be tortured?"

Terry and Nancy glanced at each other. Any second now Juarez would learn that his chances to torture Nancy or anyone else had come to an end forever.

At that moment the police leaped from the bushes, followed by Terry and Dr. Anderson. There were astonished cries, a fight, but it was over quickly. Juarez and his two accomplices were handcuffed, then the police went through their pockets.

"The black keys!" Terry cried as one of the policemen held them out. "And the half-key, too!"

Joshua Pitt's gratefulness at finally being rescued was overwhelming. Tears trickled from the elderly man's eyes.

"You are truly my friends," he said. "I should have shared the secret with you from the start."

"We understand," Terry said. "Let's forget that, and find the treasure. Where is it, Dr. Pitt?"

The professor said he had been unable to figure out the exact site, because from his translation he had learned the landmark was a tall stone shaft. According to the Indians that Juarez had consulted the evening before, this no longer existed, nor any of the other clues on the Mystery Stone.

"It may take years of digging to find the Frog Treasure," he said sadly.

Suddenly Terry snapped his fingers. "Maybe not," he said. "I believe Nancy has solved the mystery for us. She pieced the story together from the photographs I took of some drawings in that old diary which the Wangells had. Let's see—what were they, Nancy?"

Excitedly Nancy told about the footprints lead-

ing to a large pool, with a split palm tree along
its edge. Terry translated this to the police.

"*Sí, sí!*" one said, and told them to follow him.

Presently the dense growth gave way to a small
lake. There were many palm trees growing near
it.

"Look for a marker," Dr. Pitt said, new enthu-
siam taking hold of him. "Maybe that stone shaft
is only covered up. The top of it might be showing."

Everyone searched eagerly. It was Dr. Pitt who
finally located the marker. The top of the narrow
stone monument was barely visible among the
leaves and undergrowth. Into it was roughly cut
the symbol of a frog!

"This must be it!" he cried excitedly. "Let's
dig here!"

Terry took the shovel and quickly set to work
unearthing the shaft. One of the policemen stepped forward.

"Let the prisoners dig!" he ordered.

Juarez was given the shovel. When he seemed
to be lagging, the officer prodded him with his
boot. Wangell and Porterly had to take their
turns. The hole grew deeper and wider.

At last, several feet underground they came
upon a tarnished but waterproof chest of solid
silver, richly ornamented. Terry lifted it out. The
chest had three separate locks, on the front, the

back and the bottom, for each of the obsidian keys.

"I hope they work," Nancy thought fervently as Terry inserted the first one.

Terry turned it. The lock yielded. The second gave way. Fortunately, the break in the half-key was not in a vital spot and also worked.

Terry swung open the lid. The Mexicans crowded close, their eyes round with wonder.

Inside was indeed a Frog Treasure. There were frogs of various sizes, made of silver. All but a very large one were set with precious jewels: emeralds, sapphires, and turquoise.

Juarez was beside himself with rage. "It would have been our treasure," he screamed, "if it hadn't been for Nancy Drew."

Dr. Pitt eyed him contemptuously. "The treasure belongs to none of us. It is the property of the Mexican government."

"But where is the secret, Dr. Pitt?" Nancy asked. "The fabulous secret of antiquity that you say can destroy mankind?"

"It will be found," the professor replied, "inside this large silver frog."

Taking the finely carved relic in his hands, he showed the others the tiny mark where one foot of the frog had been attached. Joshua Pitt pulled off the foot. A greenish powder trickled out. He plugged the hole quickly.

"This substance," he said, "has a terrible power. We must destroy it forever."

Terry Scott was thoughtfully taking a paper from his pocket.

"Perhaps so," he said. "But I hope and believe, sir, that you are mistaken."

He showed the paper to the other scientists. It was the cryptic note containing the symbols of the frog, sun, and prostrate man.

"As you know," Terry continued, pointing to the figure of the prostrate man, "this symbolizes death. But it can also mean disease or human weakness. It must be considered in relation to the other symbols, particularly the symbol of the sun."

Joshua Pitt's eyes now had an excited, happier gleam. "Go on," he said.

"According to my interpretation," Terry said, "the frog represents the sacredness of the secret rather than a motive of evil. The secret is that this green powder can heal mankind."

"I think you're right," Dr. Anderson agreed.

For a long time Joshua Pitt studied the three symbols. At last he nodded.

"You've convinced me. This powder must be an ancient herb remedy. We'll have it analyzed."

He replaced the silver frog in the chest. Dr. Anderson picked up the treasure, and the little procession started back to civilization, where

Juarez and his friends would be imprisoned, and where the scientists would announce their find to the world.

Terry took Nancy's arm. "How does it feel," he asked, smiling, "to be such an important person? After all, it was you who finally solved this mystery."

Laughing, Nancy said she was glad that the case had ended so happily. Now she wondered when a new mystery would challenge her. A strange puzzle presented itself in a short time, *Mystery at the Ski Jump.*

"But *The Clue of the Black Keys* is not yet finished," Dr. Anderson spoke up, a twinkle in his eye. "Not until Nancy Drew has visited my classes at Clifton. I want you to tell my students, Nancy, that the best way to discover treasure is to have an observing eye and a brave heart.

"I wish all my students were live wires like Nancy Drew!"

NANCY DREW MYSTERIES